Slick 2

Brenda Hampton

www.urbanbooks.net

Urban Books, LLC
300 Farmingdale Road, NY-Route 109
Farmingdale, NY 11735

ISBN 13: 978-1-62286-546-8
ISBN 10: 1-62286-546-4

First Mass Market Printing November 2017
First Trade Paperback Printing November 2015
Printed in the United States of America

10 9 8 7 6 5 4 3 2 1

*This is a work of fiction. Any references or similar-
ities to actual events, real people, living or dead, or
to real locales are intended to give the novel a sense
of reality. Any similarity in other names, charac-
ters, places, and incidents is entirely coincidental.*

Distributed by Kensington Publishing Corp.
Submit orders to:
Customer Service
400 Hahn Road
Westminster, MD 21157-4627
Phone: 1-800-733-3000
Fax: 1-800-659-243

Slick 2

by

Brenda Hampton

People simply didn't like me. I was labeled a phony, a backstabbing bitch, and an insecure woman who was confused and cutthroat. Considering what I had done to my best friend, Dana, everybody thought I was trying to be slick. Truthfully, I wasn't. I had just fallen in love with her husband. Working for him for all those years made it so easy.

The hard part was Dana finding out about our relationship. She was crushed, but eventually got over it. I hadn't seen her since I left St. Louis. The last thing I heard was she remarried and was now living happily ever after, while spending another rich man's money. I was in no position to judge her. I had my own problems to deal with. Problems that stemmed from me being in love with the one, and only, Jonathan Taylor.

The plus side was I now had time to reflect on everything that had happened, including my mistakes. I took *some* responsibility for what I had done to hurt others. If I ever had an opportunity to see Dana again, I would tell her how sorry I was for interfering in her marriage. I would also tell her how I felt about Jonathan today. About him getting remarried and how much I wanted him back. But sharing my thoughts with her wasn't the priority. Jonathan needed to know how I felt. I wanted him to know that I was still in love with him. If his feelings were the same, I hoped that he would be willing to end his relationship with the other woman. We had deprived ourselves for too long. Maybe this was the time for us to piece back our relationship and move forward together. I wholeheartedly believed that was possible, but if it wasn't, I told myself that I was ready to move on. More so, I tried to convince myself that I was.

I paced the floor in the living room with the cell phone gripped in the palm of my sweaty hand. I wasn't sure if calling him was the right thing to do, or if a face-to-face meeting would be more appropriate. It didn't take long for me to finalize my decision, so I punched in his number and waited for him to answer. Almost immediately, the deep, masculine sound of the simple word "hello" made my stomach tighten. My mouth was open, but no words escaped.

"Hello," he said again. "Is anyone there?"

I was sure he'd heard my heavy breathing, so I quickly snapped out of my trance to respond. "Jonathan, it's me. Sylvia."

"What's up, Sylvia? I wasn't sure if I would hear from you again, but I'm glad you called. Your voice always has a way of putting a smile on my face, and I can tell you already that it has definitely been one of those rough days around here."

A Colgate smile appeared on my face. I started to feel at ease—a little. "I know how busy things can get at the office, so I surely understand. And, just so you know, hearing your voice has an effect on me as well. But, uh, I'm calling to see if we could meet somewhere and talk. I have multiple things that I need to share with you. I don't want to discuss those things over the phone."

There was a sharp silence before he responded. "Let me look at my calendar to see when I don't have much going on. Hold on a second."

As he paused, I bit my nails and continued to pace the floor.

"How about Friday? Can you meet me in the Central West End?"

Friday? That was three days away. I didn't want to appear too anxious, so I agreed to meet him. "The Central West End is fine. What about Bar Louie at six?"

"Sounds like a plan to me. I can't wait to see you again. I have a lot on my mind, too. Meanwhile, I have to run. Need to be in court in less than fifteen minutes. I'm already running late."

"I know how much you don't like to be late, so go. I'll see you soon."

"Most definitely."

Our call ended on that note. No words could express how excited I was to see Jonathan.

Friday couldn't get here soon enough. I sat on the couch, biting my nails some more and reflecting on the last time I had seen Jonathan, prior to him breaking the news to me about him getting married. That day at Lambert Airport stuck with me forever. It was difficult, as well as painful to let go.

I was standing in Burger King at the airport, thinking hard about all we'd been through. I wanted to call him to say good-bye, so I pulled out my cell phone and punched in his number. I quickly hit the end button then dialed his number again. When I listened to his phone ring, I also heard another cell phone behind me ringing. I hung up then dialed his number again. When I heard the cell phone behind me again, I quickly swung around. Jonathan was leaned against a pole with a serious look on his face. He looked like what J.J. from Good Times *would consider "dy-no-mite." Neatly dressed in a navy blue suit and wearing a long black trench coat, he made my heart melt. I turned back around and smiled so he wouldn't know how excited I was to see him. He came over and sat at the table with me.*

"I was wondering when you were going to call. I knew you were, but I tried to be patient," he said. I gazed at him then lowered my head,

as my eyes started to water. "None of that." He lifted my chin so I could look at him.

I swallowed the oversized lump in my throat then released a deep breath. "I . . . I can't help it. Do you even know what it feels like when you know that you lost a good thing? I could kill myself, Jonathan, for what I put you through."

"Hurting from a loss is kind of like what I'm feeling right now. And don't go blaming yourself because I made some major mistakes too. I should have told you about Courtney's feelings up front, but I didn't. That was my fault, and I can't blame you for acting the way you did."

"Well, you didn't tell me because I was always acting a damn fool. I should have just trusted you when you asked me to. I had no reason not to, other than me being so insecure."

"Yeah, you should have trusted me, but, it . . . it's—"

"Finish the sentence. It's not worth it anymore, is it? As much as I want to throw away this plane ticket and stay here in St. Louis to be with you, you won't let me, will you?"

Jonathan moved his head from side to side, before placing his hand on top of mine. "You need to . . . we need to move on. I have not stopped loving you not one bit, but it would be difficult for us to stay together, especially after what we've been through."

I got choked up and was so hurt that I didn't even want to respond. I knew Jonathan was right, but I still had a tough time letting go. "So, will you and Britney come see me sometimes?"

"Of course. And only if you promise to come visit us as well."

"I will. I wish you would have brought Britney with you so I could have said good-bye to her."

"I wanted to, but I knew what a tough time she'd have seeing you leave."

"Yeah, you're right. But you be sure to tell her I love her. I'll call her every day so we can talk. And, speaking of talking, have you heard from Dana?"

"Every once in a while, I do. She's got a new boyfriend and they're doing fine. Actually, I met him several weeks ago. I didn't tell you because I didn't know how—"

"How I would react, right?"

"Right."

"I really made a fool of myself, didn't I?"

He blushed while squeezing my hands together with his. "You don't want me to answer that, do you?"

I laughed and watched as he planted a soft kiss against the back of my hand.

We talked for the next hour or so as I waited for my plane to depart. He said he wasn't going to hire a new secretary, and if he did, he said it would be a minute. I asked him if he intended on dating again, but all he did was shrug his shoulders. That meant dating was still on the table, and when I told him what a lucky woman she would be, he just smiled.

The announcement of my plane's departure came over loud and clear. I stood and so did Jonathan.

"Do you have everything?" he asked.

"Just about," I said, hurtfully reaching inside of my purse for the boarding pass. I pulled it out. "There it is."

"Okay, then let me walk you to your gate. I don't think they'll let me go that far, but I'll go with you as far as I can."

Jonathan took my hand and we walked through the airport as if we were a happy couple, simply saying good-bye for a short period of time. A TSA security guard halted our steps when he asked for our boarding passes. I showed him mine, knowing that this was the farthest Jonathan could go. He kissed the back of my hand again, and knowing that he was hurting just as much as I was inside, again, I asked him if he wanted me to stay.

"Baby, all you have to do is say the word," I said, wiping a tear as it ran down my face. "I *will say to hell with Atlanta and spend the rest of my life with you. From now on, I promise I'll trust you. No more fighting and arguing. I promise you that we will figure out a way to get along better."*

I saw his Adam's apple move up and down, as he tried hard to fight back his emotions. He muffled his voice then slowly closed his eyes. When he opened them they were filled with water. He then made his final decision that left me even more distraught. "Go, please. I need you to go. I promise you that we'll keep in touch."

"But that's not good enough. I want to be with you." I reached up and grabbed the back of his head. When I pulled him forward to kiss me, he gave me a quick peck on the lips then backed away.

"Go ahead, baby, please," he begged. "You're only making this harder, and I don't want you to miss your plane."

With my entire body feeling weak and full of pain, I threw my arms around him to get one last hug. I then gave the TSA guard my boarding pass, and carried my small bag through the gates. I didn't even bother to turn around because the tears poured so rapidly down my face I could barely see. I could feel Jonathan *still watching me and silently prayed for a miracle to happen and happen fast. By the time I got on the plane, I looked around in hopes of seeing him. No luck. Minutes later, the plane got off the ground and headed for Atlanta. That's when it finally sank in that our relationship was over.*

I sighed from my thoughts of the past and prayed that Friday would be everything I imagined it to be.

Dressed to impress, I sat at Bar Louie in the Central West End, waiting for Jonathan to show. It was almost ten minutes after six. He was late. That irritated me, especially since I had gone all out for this occasion. The spaghetti-strap purple dress that I wore melted on my curves. Most of my hair was slicked back, but was curled at the tips. Several strands dangled along the sides of my face, and my gold hoop earrings matched my bangles and necklace. Plum lipstick moistened my full lips, and right before I came here, I had stopped at the MAC counter to get the hookup on my makeup and lashes. It was important for me to look my best. I was hyped, until I looked up and saw Jonathan strut into the restaurant with a woman by his side. My face twisted and my mouth fell wide open. *Didn't I tell him I wanted to speak to him, not her? How dare he bring her with him?*

The direction of my eyes traveled from the tips of her weaved-in hair to the point of her cheap-looking heels. I couldn't help but to notice how plain she was. She had no curves what-soever, her long, stringy hair had no bounce, and the heavy makeup she had on made her look casket ready. The red lip gloss did nothing for her pale skin, but I figured those big lips came in handy. There was no way in hell that she was Jonathan's type, but, then again, he did like skinny-ass, light-skinned women who resembled his ex-wife, Dana. He could definitely do better than this, though, and how dare he disrespect me by bringing her to dinner? Maybe I should have reminded him to come alone.

Since I hadn't told him, there was a knot in the pit of my stomach making me want to throw up. I wondered if he could tell how disappointed and pissed I was by looking at the tight expression on my face. As a matter of fact, I was positive that he could tell. Over the years, he'd seen the same expression plenty of times.

"Sylviaaaa," Jonathan said with a warm smile on his face as he approached me.

My heart slammed against my chest when I heard him say my name. I swear I loved this man to death. No matter how upset I was with him, this wasn't enough to wash away my feelings. The steel gray suit he wore accented his salt-and-pepper waved, flowing hair and trimmed beard. Like always, he was clean-cut, classy, and sharp as ever. His business attire was always on point, and the smell of his expensive cologne infused the entire area around us. No matter where he was, he always garnered much attention and presented himself with class.

With wet palms and shaky knees, I slowly stood to greet him. "Hello, Jonathan. I'm glad you could make it."

"So am I." His deep voice made a chill rush up my spine. "My fiancée was on her way out with some friends. I asked her to come in and meet you. Lesa, this is Sylvia."

With a fake smile on her face, she extended her hand to mine. "Nice to meet you, Sylvia. I've heard so much about you. This is such a pleasure."

Who in the hell was she trying to kid? In no way was this a pleasure. Only Lord knows what Jonathan had told her about me, but, at this point, it didn't matter. I went with the flow.

"Same here, Lesa. I haven't heard much about you, but I suspect that it's all good, especially if you're going to be Jonathan's wife."

"I definitely will be," she rushed to say. "And I must say that I'm looking forward to being the new Mrs. Taylor."

I cringed, hoping that she didn't notice the twitching in my left eye. Maybe she did, because she rolled her eyes then turned to Jonathan. She gave him a peck on the lips and winked at him.

"I'll see you later tonight. Have fun and don't forget what we discussed."

Jonathan nodded. He waved as she walked away. If I could prevent him from seeing her later tonight, I surely would.

"Well, well, well," he said as he pulled back the chair to take a seat. A smile was locked on his face. I could tell he was as happy to see me as I was to see him. "I must say, Sylvia, that you look spectacular."

"Thank you. So do you, but I would never expect anything less."

He searched into my eyes while rubbing his hands together. It appeared that he had something on his mind, but, whatever it was, he switched his attention to the menu on the table. "Let's see," he said. "What shall I order?"

"If my memory serves me correctly, I'll say you'll be ordering the stuffed chicken with broccoli, and a garden salad with an extra piece of bread. You'll wash it all down with white wine, and, for dessert, you'll consider something chocolate. What you can really have isn't on the menu. And, personally, I think what isn't on the menu may be much more fulfilling."

He laid the menu down then massaged his hands together. I guessed he was surprised by my bluntness, but he shouldn't have been.

"That sounds exactly like what I would order, but in reference to what's not on the menu, I'm not interested in that anymore, especially since I recently heard some things about you that concern me."

My brows shot up. That fast, I caught an attitude. "What exactly have you heard about me that concerns you? If Dana has shared some things with you about me, that shouldn't concern you, because you already know how she feels about me. I don't know who else could've said anything to you about me, because we don't share the same friends."

He tapped his fingertips on the table while narrowing his eyes to look at me. "Interesting. I believe that if you think real hard, you may be able to come up with a name. I'm not going to tell you his name, and you're right. He's my friend, not yours. And just so you know, I was highly disappointed to hear about your *actions*."

Okay. Now I knew where he was going with this. Jonathan had to be talking about my little sex session with Jaylin Rogers. I suspected that Jonathan would find out sooner or later, but this wasn't the conversation I wanted to have with him right now. Regardless, I had to say something and do my best to defend myself.

"I'm not surprised that he contacted you, but why does anything he says about me concern you?"

He released a deep sigh. I could sense slight anger building from the way he sucked his teeth and licked across his lips. That's what he'd done in the past whenever I said something that got underneath his skin.

"It does concern me. I didn't think you were the kind of woman to put yourself out there like that and open up your legs to anyone. Particularly, a good friend of mine who has had numerous sex partners. Not that it matters, but he didn't call me. I reached out to him about a case I was working on. Your name happened to come up. I was shocked by what he'd told me; and was it necessary for you to go down on him?"

I almost choked on the water I was drinking to stay chill. If anything, I wanted to get up and run. I couldn't believe Jaylin gave Jonathan specific details, and I was disgusted that they had been discussing me.

"To be honest, Jonathan, I don't care what Jaylin told you. I didn't come here to talk about him. I'm here to talk about us. You do remember what happened between us, don't you? If not, I can always refresh your memory about our loving relationship that, unfortunately, fell apart. We both made mistakes, and I forgive you, only if you can forgive me too."

He was blunt. "All is forgotten, and there is no need to refresh my memory because there is no us anymore. Even though you didn't come here to talk about Jaylin, I can't help but to wonder how many items you served him from your menu. I'm not happy about you having sex with him, Sylvia, and I'm not going to sit here and pretend that it's all good. I think you did it out of spite. How petty is that?"

This fool done fell and bumped his head. Or maybe Lesa had his mind twisted. How dare he get all snippy about this, especially when he was the one who had hurt me in the past? Not to mention that he had moved on and was now getting married.

With a screwed face, I crossed my legs and let him have it. "Spiteful and petty? No. I had sex with Jaylin because I needed a good lay and he has a stellar reputation when it comes to satisfying women. I figured that he would deliver, and, bravo, he did. Now, I'll repeat myself. I'm not here to talk about who I've been giving my goodies to. And while you've made it clear that there is no more us, I don't know if I believe you. The look in your eyes doesn't imply that, and you seem real jealous about what transpired between me and your friend. Is that why you brought your fiancée in here tonight? To make me jealous? If so, you failed miserably. Quite frankly, my dear, she wasn't all that."

Jonathan shrugged and remained calm. "I brought her here because I wanted you to meet her. I'm not jealous about what happened between you and Jaylin. I'm just disappointed, as well as disgusted. That's what you see in my eyes. Nothing more."

"So disappointed and disgusted that you prefer we sit here all night to discuss it? If that's the case, maybe we should wrap this up and go our separate ways. I'm sure you have other things to do with your time. I must say that I do too."

He was never the kind of man to keep up a bunch of nonsense, so I wasn't caught off guard when he stood and laid twenty dollars on the table.

"You're right. I do have better things to do with my time tonight. I don't know why I came here, especially after knowing what you did with my friend. That was low, Sylvia. I never would have done anything like that to you. I guess this was a little reminder about the kind of woman you really are."

My mouth dropped open as he walked away. *No, he didn't just go there.* I was so mad that I shot up from my chair and trailed behind him.

"It puzzles me that you still care about who I spend my time with," I softly hissed so people inside of the restaurant wouldn't suspect an argument brewing between us. Jonathan ignored me and walked so fast that I could barely keep up. By the time I did catch up to him, we were outside. I was almost out of breath, but I continued to make my point.

"Our relationship has been over with for a while. I'm not the one getting married. You are, right?"

He pivoted to face me. "Yeah, I am. And thank God the woman I'm marrying is nothing like you."

Ouch. That hurt. Regardless, I let him know that he couldn't back up his words with his hideous-looking fiancée. He needed to come again.

"By looking at your woman, I can tell she's nothing like me. What a shame that is, because I know what kind of woman excites you. I know what a woman must bring to the table to keep you happy. She didn't appear to fit the bill, and

I feel sorry for you if you're settling for someone who has nothing in common with me."

He stopped next to his black BMW and placed his hand on the handle. While I appeared totally flustered, he remained calm as ever.

"I don't do this anymore, Sylvia. Enough is enough. There's no need for us to have these kinds of confrontations, so do me a favor: don't reach out to me again, okay? You have my word that I'm going to leave this conversation right here. I've said all that I'm going to say, and I hope you've gotten some things off your chest. If not, you won't be given another opportunity to behave like this."

That was his way of calling me childish, but I refused to keep my mouth shut. "Hell, no, I haven't gotten anything off my chest, considering all you wanted to talk about was Jaylin. But have it your way, Jonathan. I have no problem not reaching out to you again. Good-bye and good luck."

Taking the high road, he got in his car and sped off. My car was nearby, so I stomped to it with disgust written all over my face. All week, I visualized us having a decent dinner, laughing and talking about old times. Then, sealing our date with a kiss. I locked in my head what I wanted to say to him about my lingering feelings.

I was so wishful that he would spill his guts and tell me that he was still in love with me too. Boy was I wrong. Wrong. Wrong. Wrong.

My high-rise apartment was only a few blocks away. I parked in the parking garage, and since my feet were killing me, I removed my high heels, carrying them in my hand. With a frown on my face, I waited for the elevator to open. When it did, I stepped inside. My head hung low, but the moment I lifted it, I saw a man's hand grab the elevator as it began to close. Within a second, Jonathan appeared. I sucked in a deep breath and held it. There was no smile on his face when he stepped forward. The elevator closed behind him and proceeded to go up.

"I was wrong," he said in a whisper. "So were you, Sylvia. Nonetheless, I didn't meet with you tonight to argue. I wanted to meet with you so I could look you in the eyes and do this."

He inched forward then reached out to hold my face. His thumbs brushed against my cheeks and our eyes locked together. The moment his lips touched mine, my heart rate increased. I sucked in another deep breath, causing my firm breasts to rise against his chest. There were no words to describe how I felt as our tongues danced together. There were no words to utter as I felt my pussy throbbing. I couldn't say one word as his hands roamed my body, squeezing me in all the right places. But the one thing that I could say was Jonathan's marriage would never happen if things were left up to me. This night belonged to us. I was hot, bothered, and ready to make every single moment count.

CHAPTER 2

LESA

I drove frantically to my destination, while gazing straight ahead. It took a lot for me to pretend as if Jonathan's meeting with Sylvia didn't worry me. It did. I wrestled with keeping my mouth shut, ever since he mentioned her phone call and her dire need to see him. He stressed, over and over again, that their relationship was a wrap. Said there was nothing wrong with a man meeting up with his ex, and he asked me if I trusted him. I did. With all of my heart I truly did, but the problem was, I didn't trust her. And after seeing her at the restaurant, I knew why. The way she looked at Jonathan said it all. She couldn't wait to dig her claws into him and was ready to eat him alive. She undressed him right in front of me, and fucked his brains out on the dining table while I witnessed it. I could sense how badly she wanted him, and it was obvious that she'd gotten dolled up just for him.

Also, the way she looked at me was alarming. She wanted me out of the picture. Her devilish gaze said so. Not to mention the slight roll of her eyes and her fake smile that made me want to puke. I wondered if Jonathan noticed her demeanor, and if he had, would he call her out on it?

He told me about her coming to his office a few weeks ago to let him know she had moved back to St. Louis. That's when he announced that we were getting married. I was thankful to him for immediately shutting things down. I was sure she had high hopes for them; she most likely assumed they would be getting back together. When he told me she left his office in tears, I wanted to laugh. Did she really think that she could just pop back into his life and he would drop everything for her? I didn't think so, and I was glad that she'd gotten her face cracked. She had no business going there to see him. A phone call would've been more appropriate. She didn't know what the hell she would walk into, and, thankfully, I wasn't there that day. She would've really gotten her feelings hurt, like they were hurt tonight.

I swear I wanted to laugh again after seeing that dumb smile on her face vanish when she saw me. Pure jealousy was in her eyes as she attempted to pick me apart. I knew I looked good, but I couldn't say the same for her. On a scale of one to ten, I gave her a six. Only because she looked as if she needed to shed a few pounds. While some men liked all those curves, I was surprised that Jonathan didn't have a problem with them. Her big breasts looked as if they were about to pop out of her dress, and when she stood, her round ass was quite noticeable. Her waist seemed fit, and that was all she really had going for her. To me, she looked as if she wanted to break down right then and there and cry. That's what was so funny. I was pleased that Jonathan had invited me to go inside with him. It let me know that he wasn't trying to keep our relationship a secret, and that he was proud to have me as his fiancée. As far as I was concerned, everything was good with him. With her, not so much.

My speeding vehicle skidded into the parking spot, almost jumping the curb. I pressed my foot on the brake then hurried to put the car in park. I took a deep breath to calm my nerves, and then snatched up my cell phone that was on the seat. I checked my text messages, hoping that Jonathan had sent me something to let me know how the night was going. His last message was from the night before. I huffed then decided to send him a quick message to see if he would respond.

Hey, handsome. Just wanted to let u know that I got here safely. After we leave here, we're going somewhere to have a few drinks. Hope you're having a good time. But be careful cause Sylvia looks as if she wants to hurt u. BAD, if you know what I mean. LOL

I sat in the car for five minutes, waiting for a response. There was no reply, so I dropped the phone in my purse then went inside of the Japanese restaurant where several of the close people I worked with awaited me. From a distance, I spotted Morgan, Sheila, Vince, Christopher, Anna, and Lance sitting on the floor in a circle with numerous silk pillows surrounding them. A chef with a tall baker's cap on was in the center, preparing a meal that sizzled from the high flames. The delicious, spicy smell went up my nostrils and signaled to my belly how hungry I was. Everyone smiled as they saw me heading their way, and when Lance patted the cushion next to him, I squatted to take a seat.

"We're so glad you finally made it," Morgan said. "You're going to love this place, and you must bring Jonathan here so he can taste the food too."

Speaking of Jonathan, I quickly opened my purse to check my phone and see if he had responded to my text. He hadn't, so I texted him again:

The food in this place looks delicious. I want u to come here with me. When do u think you'll have time?

This time, I directed a question to him so that he could reply. All it took was seconds to respond, but as the night went on, I didn't receive one text. I wasn't sure if anyone had noticed my somber mood, until Lance stopped me as I was coming out of the restroom. He reached for my hand, holding it with his.

"Tell me," he said, moving my hair away from my sad eyes. "What's wrong? Normally, you're upbeat and a true delight to be around. Tonight is different. Are you okay?"

I swallowed the lump in my throat while looking down at the ground. The last thing I wanted to do was spill my guts to Lance. I knew how much he liked me; he had always liked me.

But it wasn't in my best interest to get caught up in a love triangle with me, him, and Jonathan. I loved Jonathan, and, thus far, I had no reason whatsoever to seek attention from another man.

Lance lifted my chin, making me look into his sexy brown eyes that were slightly slanted. His full lips resembled Tyson Beckford's, and so did his nicely cut frame that was stacked with bulging muscles.

"Speak," he said. "I'm here as a friend, and you can always tell me what you're going through. I said it before and I'll say it again. If things don't work out between you and your man, I'm always here."

I released my hand from his. "Things are working out just fine. I appreciate your thoughtfulness, but stop assuming that something is wrong with my relationship when there isn't."

"Sure. If you say so. But if there ain't nothing wrong, why do you keep looking at your phone? Why do you keep staring off into space, and why haven't you eaten anything tonight? You can say what you wish, but I can tell that something is bothering you. I won't press, but you already know that what one man won't do, another one certainly will."

Lance was trying to confuse the situation. I had no reason to run to him. Jonathan would never betray me, and that I was sure of. Sure of for at least another hour or so. He still hadn't replied to my text, and this had never happened before.

By the time I left the restaurant, I was livid. I sat in the car with my head pressed against the steering wheel. My throat ached and my heart was heavy. I couldn't stop visualizing what was going on tonight where he couldn't return my call or simply reply to my text. Did Sylvia get what she wanted from him? Did he now have a change of heart about us? My thoughts were all over the place, but they were interrupted by Lance as he pulled on the handle to open the door. He squatted beside me.

"You say nothing is wrong, but you declined to go have drinks with us. That's not like you. You look as if you're in a daze, and all I'm asking is for you to tell me what's going on with you. It feels good to get things off your chest. I'm only here to help you, not hurt you."

That was good to know. I turned toward Lance and started to spill my guts and tell him how I felt about Jonathan meeting up with Sylvia. My lips quivered as I spoke about their past relationship. I could only recall what Jonathan had told me, and it was enough to let me know that they had been deeply in love with each other.

After speaking about it, it wasn't long before my emotions took over. Lance leaned in to give me a squeezing hug.

"Don't assume anything about the two of them," he said. "Let the chips fall where they may, but please know that if you fall, I will catch you. Now, wipe those tears from that pretty face and let's get out of here."

With that kind of support, how could I resist?

CHAPTER 3

JONATHAN

Sylvia was definitely back. I didn't quite know how to handle it, but I was sure of one thing. My love for her had dissipated, partially because of what she had done with Jaylin, but mainly because I was in love with someone else. Lesa meant everything to me. We'd been together for the past two years. I hadn't cheated on her, until last night. I wasn't sure why I had gone there with Sylvia, but a big part of me wanted to go there again, just to see if my love for her rekindled. It didn't. The sex was spectacular, but it wasn't enough to move me. I needed more from a woman, and Sylvia wasn't where I needed her to be. She still seemed confrontational, and, during dinner, I could tell she hadn't changed much.

According to her, she was going to start working as Crissy Duncan's assistant on Monday.

Crissy was the daughter of one of my deceased partners. She had done a good job filling his shoes at the law firm. Thus far, she had done rather well for herself. She and Sylvia had gotten close over the years, and Crissy seemed to have her back. There was a time when they hated each other, couldn't get along for nothing in the world, but Crissy came through for Sylvia when she needed someone to lean on.

I didn't think that Sylvia working at the firm again would be a problem, especially since Crissy's office was way on the other side of the building. Besides, I spent less time in the office, more time at home. Lesa preferred to have it that way. She was the one who had hired several interior decorators to hook up my home office, and she seriously took care of me, with few complaints. Dinner was always on the table, the house stayed sparkling clean, and, on top of that, she continued to pursue her career as a fashion designer. I appreciated an ambitious woman, one who could take care of herself and her man at the same time. There was no question that I was lucky to have her, and I was sure to keep what had happened between me and Sylvia on lock. If Lesa ever found out, that would surely be the end of us.

The last time the cat got out of the bag was because of my daughter, Britney. She was the one who told Dana I'd been with Sylvia, simply because she wanted Sylvia and me together. Thankfully, Britney was away at college now, pursuing a law degree. I barely heard from her these days. Whenever we spoke, our conversations were very brief. I believed that her boyfriend had something to do with that as well. The one thing I had learned over the years was not to push. As long as she was happy, so was I.

While thinking about Britney, I sat in my home office with my chair leaned back and my feet propped on the desk. I was still in my pajamas, and had taken a quick shower when I arrived home at three in the morning. Lesa had gone out with her friends. She didn't get home until almost four, but had texted me several times throughout the evening. I hadn't replied because my phone was turned off. I was glad that I had made it home before she had. I wasn't expecting her to question me, but when I looked up and saw her coming into my office, the first question she asked was what time did I get home.

I scratched my waves then removed my feet from the desk. Hated to lie, but in this case, I had to. Things had been going well for us. The last thing I wanted was for Lesa to feel some kind of way about Sylvia. Lesa knew a lot about our past. Basically, I told her everything from how things got started to how they ended. When I mentioned my meeting with Sylvia, Lesa gave me her approval.

"I got home a little after midnight," I said. "I saw your text messages a few hours ago, but my phone had been turned off since my business meeting earlier. I forgot to turn it back on. Bar Louie was crowded and it took a long time before we got service. Plus, Sylvia kept running her mouth about things that don't really matter much anymore. We're on the same page now, and I want to thank you for not having a problem with me meeting her."

Lesa didn't reply. She just stood in all of her sexiness, gazing at me. She was thirty-nine, seven years younger than I was. Her hair was swept into a long ponytail that revealed her round face and deep-set, mysterious eyes. While in her gray silk robe, I watched as she strutted around my desk to sit on my lap. Her arms fell on my shoulders and she leaned in for a juicy kiss. I hoped the taste of Sylvia's pussy wasn't still stirring in my mouth.

"Mmmm," she moaned then backed away and licked her full lips. "That's what I was missing this morning. Breakfast is almost done, so I expect for you to join me in about fifteen more minutes. That's unless you have something else in mind."

She started to undo the buttons on my pajama shirt. I was exhausted from fucking Sylvia; no question she wore me out. I didn't have much energy to tackle Lesa right now, so I reached for her hand, kissing the back of it.

"I'm working on finalizing an important case next week. Let me get a few things done, and then I'll meet you in the kitchen for breakfast. I'll tell you what's on my mind later tonight."

She kissed my cheek then smiled. "Okay, Mr. Busy Man. Don't let breakfast get cold, and I can't wait for tonight. Cherry and I have something real exciting waiting for you."

Cherry was the nickname she'd given her pussy. Any other time I'd be eager to see what was waiting. Today I wanted to pass.

She removed her arms from my shoulders then stood. As she made her way to the door, I felt guilty. I hoped that Sylvia and I would be able to keep our distance. While my feelings were not the same for her, I had to admit that sex between us always stirred up something inside of me.

Twenty minutes later, I was at the kitchen table eating breakfast with Lesa. Four pancakes were stacked high on my plate, along with two sausages and a side of cheese eggs. Diced potatoes with onions were in a bowl, and a tall glass of orange juice was in my hand. I lifted the glass, but didn't tilt it to my lips because Lesa switched our conversation to Sylvia.

"For whatever reason, I didn't think she'd be that pretty. I also didn't think she'd be that fat, and I thought she'd be some kind of ghetto queen with false lashes and a head full of weave."

"Fat? She weighs about one-seventy, and in no way is she fat. And why would you think that she's a ghetto queen? Ghetto queens aren't my type."

"Maybe not a ghetto queen to you, but for a woman to stoop as low as she did with her best friend, and to rush into a courtroom and throw a tantrum, it surely sounds like a ghetto queen to me. As for the weight thing, one-seventy is kind of up there, but I don't believe she weighs that. More like two hundred plus."

These kinds of attacks irritated me. I didn't want to spend my time with Lesa defending Sylvia, but she was saying things that weren't true.

"I don't know exactly how much she weighs, but most men appreciate how she looks. There is no question that we had some trust issues back then. She was upset, and the courtroom was where she'd found me. I don't see what that has to do with a person being ghetto."

The truth: I was furious with Sylvia that day. She clowned in the courtroom, and her actions caused me to pull away from our relationship.

Lesa bit into a piece of bacon while eyeing me from across the table. I lowered my head to cut into my pancakes.

"It sounds like you're defending her. Why would you defend such a foolish act, and also defend a woman who had sex with one of your friends? What kind of woman stoops that low and fucks your friend?"

In that moment, I realized that I had been running my mouth too much. Sometimes, being open about past relationships wasn't such a good thing.

"I'm not defending her, and she's free to have sex with whomever she wishes. All I'm saying is she's not a ghetto queen, as you say. I'm more so defending myself because I don't date women of that caliber."

She was annoying the hell out of me without even knowing it. Especially when she shrugged then bit into another piece of bacon. Her gaze made me uncomfortable. It was as if she could read me. As if she could visualize my dick sliding in and out of Sylvia last night. As if she felt my hands massaging Sylvia's thick breasts and my lips placing delicate pecks against her thighs and pussy. Maybe Lesa had heard the way Sylvia screamed my name and told me how much she still loved me after each orgasm. Lesa's look said she was on to something.

"So, what did she say?" Lesa asked. "You never told me how the conversation went last night."

I had to quickly rid myself of the guilty look that was taking over. Instead of sitting slumped in the chair, I sat up straight. I looked across the table at Lesa with wide eyes then cleared my throat.

"I didn't think it was necessary for me to provide specifics, but I did tell you that we are now on the same page. I told her that I am in love, and that you and I will be getting married soon. She mentioned her new job and expressed how excited she is to be back in St. Louis. That was pretty much it."

"Where is her new job?"

I surely didn't want to answer this, but Lesa would find out sooner or later. "At my firm."

Her brows shot up. "Your firm? Is she working for you again?"

"No. She's working for Crissy Duncan."

"Oh. I see."

The direction of Lesa's eyes shifted toward the window. She gazed outside, as if she were in deep thought. I hated that she felt uncomfortable about all of this. I had to assure her that Sylvia wouldn't be a problem.

"You've never questioned me like this before. Wha—"

She cut me off and snapped. "And I can't recall a time when I wasn't able to reach you. It was the wrong time to have your phone off, and I'm still waiting for you to reply to my text messages."

"I apologize for the phone incident, but you already know that there have been plenty of times when I've had to turn that thing off. It's a distraction in the courtroom, and I don't have it on when I'm in meetings. I simply forgot that it was off. Regardless, I want to be clear about one thing. It is over between Sylvia and me. There is nothing for you to worry about. After our dinner last night, I doubt that I'll be hearing from her again. We both agreed to go our separate ways. She knows where I stand; I know where she stands. The question is, do you know where you stand? I hope so."

Lesa's eyes shifted back to me. "I am well aware of where I stand. And as long as you know, that's all that matters."

She lifted her glass of orange juice, slightly tilting it as if we were toasting. Her eyes searched deeper into mine as she sipped from the glass, and, unfortunately for me, I could sense that she saw straight through my bullshit. In order for me to make her feel number one again, I had some major work to do.

Later that night, I had just wrapped up a phone conversation with Jaylin, who reached out to me about a legal matter that could cost him a fortune. I gave him some advice, and it wasn't long before our conversation led to what had happened between him and Sylvia. I hated to inquire, but I backed off of the conversation when he seemed as if he didn't want to share any info. There was no question that I was jealous. I didn't want either of them to know how pissed I really was.

For now, I focused on the important things like my woman. Lesa had returned from a fashion show that she had been planning for months. Per our phone conversation earlier, she was hyped about the turnout, and she couldn't wait to get home to tell me all about it. As she busted through the double doors to our bedroom, I lay in bed, rocking nothing but my chocolate skin.

A trail of pink and red rose petals made a pathway to the bed, soothing music echoed in the background, the fireplace was lit, and a bottle of chilled champagne was on the nightstand for us to celebrate her success. I had also gotten her a gift that was wrapped in gold shimmery paper and topped with a big white bow. A wide smile appeared as she stepped farther into the room, observing her surroundings.

"I thought you'd never get here," I said with a super-hard dick on display.

She stepped out of her heels then crawled her way up to me from the edge of the bed. Our tongues danced for a while before I lifted her fitted dress, exposing her nakedness. She was fit in every possible way. Had just enough curves to excite me, and I didn't mind that her breasts were much smaller than Sylvia's.

"I love it when you lay your hands on me," she whispered then laid her hands on me. Unfortunately, my dick had backed down from the excitement, leaving me hanging.

"What's wrong?" Lesa said while stroking my limp meat. "From what I saw at the door, you were good to go."

To say I was embarrassed was an understatement. This had never happened to me before.

I touched myself to see if that would help me rise to the occasion, but it didn't do much good. Lesa frowned. Disappointment washed across her face. I rolled on top of her, hoping that if I brushed my dick against her wet slit, it would help. It didn't.

"I . . . I don't know what to say. Maybe I need to go see my doctor."

"Maybe so. Let me see what I can do about this little problem."

This time, Lesa lay on top of me. She eased down low, and then wiggled my dick with her hand. Her warm mouth covered it, and she tried to suck it in to the back of her throat. It didn't budge. I closed my eyes, thinking about having sex with her and about what had transpired between Sylvia and me last night. The thoughts may have increased my package a little, but not by much. Lesa tightened her jaws, but there still wasn't much to swallow. I kept my eyes closed, just to prevent myself from looking into hers.

"You may need that doctor after all," she said, giving up. She moved next to me in bed, turning her back toward me. "Good night," she said. "Maybe next time."

I moved in close to her, wrapping my arms around her waist.

"I'm sorry," I whispered.

She didn't reply. We both lay silent. My thoughts had been all over the place tonight, and I should've known better than to try to kick up something in the bedroom with Lesa. I couldn't stop thinking about Sylvia having sex with Jaylin. I felt more betrayed by her than I did by him. She shouldn't have gone there. I kept thinking about the impact she would have on my relationship with Lesa, and the guilt from having sex with Sylvia was eating me alive. Hopefully, I'd feel better in another day or two, but, for now, any attempts to get my dick hard again failed.

I kissed Lesa's cheek then squeezed her tightly in my arms.

"I don't know what's wrong, baby, but I will absolutely find out something from my doctor. You aren't upset with me, are you?"

Lesa shrugged but didn't bother to reply. I took that as a definite *hell, yes*. It was clear as ever that she was mad as hell.

CHAPTER 4

SYLVIA

Talk about somebody doing the happy dance—that would be me. I had been on a serious high ever since Jonathan left my place early Saturday morning. I hadn't heard from him, but we both agreed to take this one day at a time. He seemed to really care about Lesa, and even though I didn't want to interfere, I had to.

Jonathan was, and had always been, my kind of man. He was the one I intended to spend my life with, and I couldn't respect his relationship with another woman. Especially one he had only known for a couple of years. We had a long history together, and our connection couldn't be ignored. I know it sounded cruel, but what kind of woman didn't fight for what she wanted?

My first day at work was an exciting one. It had been a long time since I stepped foot into the law offices of Duncan, Taylor & Bradford. I was glad to be back. Never in my wildest dreams did I think Crissy and I would be working together. Never did I think she would ultimately become my best friend. We'd kept in touch over the years, and she visited me on numerous occasions in Atlanta, where I worked for her uncle. I told her that our friendship meant the world to me. I would do everything possible not to let our closeness interfere with work.

I sat in her office, dressed in a hot-pink skirt that showed off my chocolate smooth legs. My multicolored blouse was cut low, revealing a small portion of my cleavage. A gold belt was wrapped around my waist, matching my high heels and accessories. With my hair parted down the middle and hanging a few inches past my shoulders, I felt like a million bucks. Crissy complimented my look as she sat behind her desk, sliding lip gloss against her lips. After the plastic surgery, her lips were fuller, breasts were bigger, and ass was that of a Kardashian. Her super-long blond hair was beautiful, though, and her blue eyes were enough to steal any man's heart.

"And even though you look fabulous today," she said, "we can't let our friendship interfere, so get out of here and get back to work. I have so much for you to do, and I couldn't wait to fire that lazy trick who was getting paid for nothing. So, glad you're back, and don't forget to let me know what time you want to schedule your lunch for. I'll be in and out all day. You already know how to reach me."

"I do. I'll let you know about lunch. As for the trick thing, why would you talk about that woman like that? She seemed nice whenever I called here. You should be ashamed of yourself for speaking so ill of her."

Crissy smacked her lips together. "Honey, calling her a trick is putting it mildly. I could call her much more than that, but I won't. She had the hots for Mr. Jonathan Taylor, and I'm sure you already know that's a no-no around here."

"Yes, it is, and you did the right thing by firing her. How dare that trick try to go there with my man?"

We laughed. She closed her purse then crossed her legs. "So. Have you heard from him since you've been back?"

"Yes, I have, but now isn't the time or place to discuss this. I'm here to work. We can chat later."

Crissy giggled then waved her hands in the air as if she'd won the lottery. She then calmed herself and leaned closer to whisper. "Oh my God. You're fucking him again, aren't you? Are you really screwing him again already?"

I rolled my eyes at her. "No, I'm not screwing him again. He's engaged, and I refuse to interfere."

She rolled her eyes too. "Whatever. That hussy he's engaged to means nothing to him. You, my dear, are the love of his life. You'd better jump on it before it's too late."

I couldn't agree with her more, but I didn't want to put my business regarding me and Jonathan out there just yet. Crissy hurried out of the chair and rushed to the door. After she closed it, she returned to her chair.

"Just so you know, I'm the boss. And the boss can always tell when employees are being untruthful. From that bright smile on your face, I can tell that you may have done more than just talk to him. So, let's start this over again. I want all of the details, quick, quick, quick."

I kept smiling and shook my head. Crissy was too much. "Look, Miss Boss Lady. I'm not going to sit here and spend the next hour or so gossiping with you. I came here to work, and I want to earn every bit of that fifty-five thousand dollars you're paying me a year."

"Fifty-five!" she shouted. "No, no, sweetheart. I said forty-five and you agreed to it."

"Never. I'm worth so much more than that, and we both determined that fifty-five would do the trick. Remember? 'Cause if you don't, you already know what's up."

Crissy laughed. "You're right. At fifty-five thousand, we don't have time to talk. Go get some work done and stay out of Mr. Taylor's way."

"Will do," I said then left her office.

Fifteen minutes later, as I was straightening things on my desk, Crissy exited her office. She informed me that she was leaving for the day.

"Be careful and keep your phone on just in case I need you," I said.

She waved good-bye as she trotted away, looking like a dolled-up hooker. Her skirt was very short, breasts looked as if they were about to break away from the tight silk blouse she wore, and her heels were at least five or six inches. She was good at what she did, though, and many of her clients praised her for getting the job done.

By noon, my desk was organized and open for business. There were so many new faces around. I had only introduced myself to Mr. Brennan Bradford's secretary and to one of the men in the mailroom. The human resources director, Pauline, stopped by to say hello. Other than that, I kept to myself. Getting involved with so many people in the workplace wouldn't benefit me at all. I learned that from the past, so I got busy on some of the work Crissy had left for me to do.

Jonathan, of course, was on my mind. I surely thought that, by now, he'd stop by to say hello. He hadn't, and I felt disappointed. I figured he was busy, but damn. All it took was five measly minutes to come this way and say hello. A phone call wouldn't hurt either, but I hadn't gotten one of those either. To say I was a little perturbed would be putting it mildly, and after another hour or so had passed by, I finally decided to make my way across the building and to his office.

As I neared it, I saw his secretary. She was an older white woman with gray long hair and black-framed glasses. Kind of reminded me of Mrs. Doubtfire. I laughed to myself, thinking about my disagreements with Jonathan in the past, when I demanded that he didn't hire a young, cute secretary after I stopped working for him. It was good to see that he was continuing to do the right thing.

Instead of going straight to his door, which was shut, I stopped at his secretary's desk. She looked up at me then smiled.

"I love the blouse," she said, paying me a compliment. "So bright and pretty."

"Thank you. I purchased it on sale at Macy's. I don't always like bright colors, but I couldn't resist."

"Good choice. I take it that you're looking for Mr. Taylor."

"Yes, I am. Is he available?"

"I'm not sure. He was on a conference call about thirty minutes ago, but let me check to see if he's finished. If so, what's your name?"

"Sylvia. He knows me."

She buzzed Jonathan's office, and after telling him my name, he told her it was okay for me to come in. I thanked her then opened the door to his office. Almost immediately, my knees weakened at the sight of his rich chocolate skin and alluring brown eyes. The dark brown tailored suit he rocked fit his frame perfectly, and the gray in his hair and beard made him appear so manly and sophisticated. His macho cologne infused the entire office. The smell made me want to take off my panties and throw them at him. I was all smiles, but unfortunately for me, he wasn't.

"I know you're busy, but I just wanted to stop in to say hello," I said.

He shot me a hard stare, appearing to have something on his mind. He then invited me to have a seat, but I wasn't sure if stopping by was a good move. I wasn't in the best mood, and apparently, he wasn't either. There was a chance that things could get heated, and I definitely didn't want that.

I took a seat in front of his desk then crossed my legs. His eyes scanned them, before his eyes connected with mine.

"How's your day going so far?" he asked.

"So far, it's going okay," I lied in order to keep the peace. "Crissy left earlier, but she left me with enough work to keep me busy."

"That's good. I hope everything works out for the two of you."

"I think they will. And the work thingy would have worked out for us too, if we hadn't gotten involved. You have to admit that I was a pretty darn good administrative assistant."

"The best. Always the best at what you do."

I couldn't help but to smile at his compliment, only because I knew he wasn't just referring to my work skills.

"Thank you. You're the best too."

He nodded then opened a drawer next to him. After looking at a piece of paper, he laid it on his desk then shifted his attention back to me. Before speaking, he cleared his throat then licked across his lips.

"I'm glad you stopped by, because I wanted to tell you something. I'm not sure about us anymore, and I'm starting to regret what happened between us the other night. Lesa has been nothing but the best woman any man could ask for. It didn't make me feel good to lie to her. I'm sure you understand where I'm going with this, don't you?"

I took a hard swallow because I didn't understand. He needed to be clearer. "No, I don't get it. You've never been the kind of man who's afraid to speak his mind, so say what you need to say and be done with it. On Friday, we agreed to approach this one day at a time. I'm not asking you to walk away from Lesa and tell her to go to hell because Sylvia's back in town. What I'm asking you to do is go where your heart is. If that's with me, fine. If not, I'm okay with that, too. But the last thing I want you to do is settle. Be happy, and be with who makes you feel at your best."

I stood then paraded to the door. I turned to him before opening it. "When you're ready to talk, you have my address, phone number, and you do know where I work. The next move is yours."

I left, feeling slightly offended by Jonathan's words, but standing by mine. The next move would have to come from him. The last thing I intended to do was chase after him. I wanted him to realize just how much he needed me back in his life. In due time, he would see that.

Instead of returning to my desk, I headed to lunch. I grabbed a quick bite to eat at Friday's, and, soon after, returned to the office. Just as I was coming out of the ladies' restroom, I bumped into Jonathan. He was strutting down the narrow hallway with several papers in his hand. His walk was pimp-like smooth, and that serious look on his face made him look mysterious and even more attractive. He nudged his head toward another hallway, and when I turned the corner, I definitely knew where he was going. We had been there numerous times before: in a spacious closet where the custodians kept several floor buffing machines, mops, and push brooms.

I followed Jonathan then moved aside as he closed the door behind me. The lights went out and the closet was now pitch black.

"I don't have all of the answers right now, and I refuse to make you any promises," he whispered. "All I know is you look damn good today. You told me to make the next move, so I'm making it."

The papers that were in his hands went up in the air then hit the floor. Within seconds, my skirt was hiked up above my waist, and my back was against the wall. My legs were wrapped around his waist as he ground deep inside of me. I couldn't even describe how I felt when his dick kept hitting my G-spot, but I tore into my lips to muffle my moans. My wetness covered his entire shaft, and the sounds of my juices popping sounded off loud and clear. Without even inquiring, he could tell I loved every bit of this. I neared an orgasm, so I wrapped my arms tightly around his neck and scratched at his flowing waves. My back squirmed against the wall, and my mouth quickly covered his. A sloppy, wet kiss was exchanged, before he lowered my legs and snatched my blouse open. My left breast popped out, giving him a hint to suck it. He did, and the heat in the closet rose to a higher temperature. Between the orgasm and breast sucking, I could barely catch my breath.

"No . . . no words can express how much I miss you. I miss this, Jonathan, and I will do everything within my power to get you back where you belong."

He didn't have to say a thing, because, thus far, I was off to a good start. I wanted him to know how I felt; maybe it would speed things along. He released my breast, but before he could tackle the other one, I fell to my knees. His pants were still at his ankles, and his hard muscle was right at my face. I opened my mouth wide, causing things to heat up again. He stroked my mouth, forcing his long goodness far down my throat. I loved the taste of him, and on my first day of work, I went into some serious overtime to make him nut. He gripped the back of my hair, squeezing it. His moans, as well as his words, pleased me more than he would ever know.

"No one isssss . . . is better at this than you," he whined. "Welcome back, baby. It's good to have you back."

I appreciated a man who knew how to clean up his act the way Jonathan did. That mess he'd said in his office went in one ear and out the other. Damn right he was glad I was back. He knew, like I did, that it didn't get much better than this.

After thirty long minutes in the closet, we walked out, hoping that no one saw or heard us. My hair was messy, clothes were wrinkled, and pussy was leaking. Jonathan looked as if he had indulged in something heavy too, but, thankfully, the coast was clear. I stole a quick kiss before we went our separate ways.

CHAPTER 5

JONATHAN

Shit. Shit. Shit. That wasn't supposed to happen, but with Sylvia looking so damn good, I couldn't help myself. Plus, I couldn't stop thinking about what had happened between Lesa and me the other night. I didn't know if my dick wouldn't cooperate because of her, or because of me. I was getting older, and sometimes men had these little problems. I figured that if Sylvia would be able to help me get it up, then there was nothing on my end. She kept it live. Live as ever. I guessed it was now time for me to stop making excuses and stop pretending that she didn't move me when she damn well did.

The sad part about all of this was I thought I was ready to settle down again. I was a much better man when I felt as if my feet were on the ground, home was safe, and my woman was happy. I didn't like playing these kinds of games with people's hearts, but I couldn't tell Lesa that I still had desires for my ex. I barely wanted to admit that shit myself, and damn Sylvia for coming back when everything with me had been going so smoothly. Yet again, we found ourselves in a messed-up situation. I was the man in the middle, confused as hell. I hated this, only because I knew that I couldn't sustain this kind of life. This wasn't me, and with the help of Lesa, I thought I had become a better man.

For the next few hours, I was in and out while listening to a witness on the stand who talked about her abusive boyfriend, Tone Pinkston. I was his lawyer. I knew he was a lowdown, dirty dog, but I took his case because of money. He was loaded, and with his parents being filthy rich, he felt entitled. Entitled to kick women's asses and make them do what he wished. I couldn't stand him, but when it came to my business, all that mattered was my bank account.

After the prosecutor finished questioning the teary-eyed woman, I stepped around the table and went after her. While she was definitely a victim, she was a gold digger, too. I started by digging into her past and making her admit to the numerous times she claimed to be assaulted by her lovers.

"I mean, this isn't the first time you've been here, is it?" I queried.

Her eyes shifted to the prosecutor, and she attempted to play dumb. "Wha . . . what do you mean? I don't understand your question."

"What I mean is you told my client that you would make all of this go away if he paid you one million dollars, didn't you?"

She moved her head from side to side. "No, I never told him anything like that. I never said anything of the sort to anyone."

"I don't want you to perjure yourself on the witness stand, and I must inform you that there are cell phone records that tell the whole story. Either you come clean now or face dire consequences later."

With more tears streaming down her face, she hesitated to speak. There was a crisp silence before she spoke up and admitted to making up the whole thing. This case had been a waste of some people's time, but it was clear to me from the beginning that this woman was after something. Tone was unquestionably full of it, but this time he was the one being played.

I stood in the hallway with Tone and his parents, after the judge dismissed the case.

"We can't thank you enough," his mother said with tears at the rims of her eyes. "I knew something wasn't right with that trick."

This time, everything worked in their favor. I was sure that Tone's parents would need my assistance again, and they would defend him no matter what. His father thanked me as well, and after they walked off, I headed to my car. From a distance, I saw a piece of paper stuck behind the windshield wiper. I snatched it off then opened the paper to read it.

YOU SLICK, DIRTY BASTARD! YOU WILL PAY, was written in red ink. Wondering who the letter was from, and who could've been watching me, I looked around the parking garage to see if I saw anyone suspicious. The letter made me real uneasy, so I quickly hopped in the car and reached for my cell phone to call Lesa. She answered with a laugh.

"These chicks are crazy!" she said. "I don't know why I watch this mess, but these Atlanta housewives be tripping."

"I don't see how you watch that stuff. Too much craziness and drama."

"Yeah, well, it's my guilty pleasure. I just got home and didn't want to miss it. You may want to stop and pick up something for dinner. I haven't had time to cook a thing."

"I'll stop to get something. Are you hungry too?"

"I am, but I'll pass on the fast food. I'll grab some fruit or something."

"You need more than fruit, don't you?"

"What I need is for my man to hurry home and give me something that I've been waiting on since our little issue the other night. Do you think you can handle that?"

"Of course. I'll be there shortly."

The note didn't appear to come from Lesa. She seemed as if everything was okay. The only other person who came to mind was Sylvia. She wasn't upset about anything, and when I called her, that was confirmed.

"I thought you were calling to see if I was home," she said. "It would be nice if you could stop by, but I'm sure you're probably tired. If so, I'll massage your back for you and wash you down real good so you can relax. All you have to do is let me know when to expect you."

"I am tired. Had a busy yet interesting day. I just wrapped up a court case, so I'm heading home to get some rest in my bed. It's been waiting for me all day, so we'll have to catch up another time. I won't be in the office until Thursday. Maybe we can do lunch or something."

"Awww. But okay. It sounds like a plan to me. Get some rest and we'll talk soon."

Our conversation confirmed that Sylvia wasn't the one who had written the note either.

Hell, maybe somebody put the paper on the wrong car. *Slick bastard* didn't apply to me, so I crumpled the paper in my hand then tossed it out the window. I drove home, listening to one of my favorite jazz players blow his horn.

I entered the house a little after nine o'clock. Lesa was in the kitchen standing in front of the stove. I hadn't stopped to get anything to eat, so I walked up from behind her to see what was cooking.

"Grits?" I said, startling her.

She jumped then turned around, holding her chest. "You scared the shit out of me. I didn't even hear you come in."

"I saw you gazing out the window. What's on your mind and why are you cooking grits this late? I didn't even know you liked them."

"I do. And what's the big deal with me cooking grits?"

I moved away from her then walked to the fridge. Maybe it was just me, feeling a little paranoid. Kind of thought she was cooking them to throw on me.

"No big deal," I said. "If that's what you want to eat tonight, fine. I'm opting for a TV dinner."

Lesa laughed and continued to stir the grits. I told her I had to take care of a few things in my office and would see her in the bedroom in a few.

By then, maybe she would be asleep. I wasn't sure if I would be able to perform for her tonight, especially after what had happened between Sylvia and me earlier. The last thing I wanted was to embarrass myself in the bedroom again.

I closed the door then sat back in the chair behind my desk. The red light on my phone was blinking, alerting me that I had several messages. One by one I listened to them. Jaylin called again, this time telling me that it was urgent for me to call him back, so I did.

"John-John, what's up?" he said.

"Not much. Same story, different day. Got your call and wanted to hit you back before I called it a night."

"I'm glad you returned my call, because I need a favor. A friend of mine's son got into some slight trouble at school. The police found drugs in his car, but he claims that they planted it there. With all that's going on in the Lou, as well as around the nation, we know that this is a possibility. The family doesn't have much money, but I want you to talk to the young man. His name is Taye. See where his head is. Tell me if you think he's guilty. You know how to read muthafuckas, and if you believe his story, I would like for you to take his case. You know I'll take care of the fees, as long as they're reasonable."

I couldn't help but to laugh at his cheap ass. "My fees are never reasonable, but you already know that. I should have some time on Thursday or Friday to pay him a visit, so shoot me his information through text. After I speak to him, I'll give you my take on things."

"That's all I ask. We'll holla sometime next week when I come to St. Louis. You can give me your thoughts then."

"Sounds good. Just let me know what day you're coming and where you'll be staying. I can't keep up with you. The last time we spoke, you mentioned buying another house here."

"It's a wrap. Done deal, and I'll take you to see it when I get there. You already know what neighborhood it's in, and no matter how many places I have, you know the Lou is home. Having a place there is a must."

"I feel you. Can't wait to see it. I doubt that it's better than mine, and I'll be sure to hook you up with my interior decorator."

"No, thanks. If it's the same one who hooked up that piece of shit-ass place you're living in right now, I'll pass."

We both laughed and couldn't resist the competition we always had. "My new interior decorator is in the kitchen right now cooking grits. I'll be sure to tell her what you said about her style."

"Cooking grits? Man, you'd better hurry up and get the fuck out of there. Any woman cooking grits at this time of the night is up to something. What in the hell did you do to her?"

I wanted to laugh but couldn't. Why? Because it was the same thing I had been thinking. It was a little too late to be cooking grits. Something wasn't right. I wanted to tell Jaylin about the letter, but I decided not to.

"I didn't do anything to her. She was craving grits, and it's probably a sign of her being pregnant. You know I've wanted another child ever since Dana lost our baby. Britney is my only child, and I wish I had more. My legacy is important."

"I definitely feel you there, but you won't have no legacy if those grits stick to that pot and start thickening. I guess you'll tell me what you did when I get there. Until then, sleep with one eye open and have your Glock real close."

Jaylin laughed then hung up. I didn't see shit funny, so I hurried to check my e-mails then went back to the kitchen. Lesa wasn't in there, but the pot was still on the stove. I lifted the top but dropped it on the floor when I heard her voice behind me.

"Got you," she said, laughing. "That was payback for scaring me earlier. Is the top still hot? I was waiting on the grits to cool. You should try some. They're real good."

"Uh, no. No, thanks. I'ma go take a shower and chill."

I walked to the bathroom while looking at Lesa from the corner of my eye. She opened the cabinet to get a bowl then worked on adding sugar and butter in the grits. I entered the master suite then the bathroom. Locked the door, just to be sure she didn't come inside. Thankfully, by the time I left the bathroom, Lesa had fallen asleep on the couch while reading a book. I was relieved—for the moment.

CHAPTER 6

LESA

I could feel everything slipping away. I didn't have any solid evidence that Jonathan had been cheating on me, but boy did I feel it. Everything about him was different. His walk, his talk, his clothes, his attitude . . . everything! Many of those things were a sign that the man I loved was losing interest in me. He was pretending. Pretending that this thing between us could magically work out, when he knew darn well that opening the door for Sylvia again would destroy us.

At this point, though, I wasn't sure what to do. I had a lot to lose, and I refused to hand Jonathan over to Sylvia on a silver platter. My intentions were to fight for my man, but I would only fight if he came clean about what was really going on. Some way or somehow, I needed to force the truth out of him. I wanted to hear straight from the horse's mouth what exactly he'd been doing with Sylvia. I wanted to know how he truly felt about her, and I needed to know for sure if marriage was something he really wanted.

Day in and out, I contemplated what to do. I had to know where his head was, so I came up with a plan that would put him on the spot, and hopefully, get him to reveal everything to me.

Jonathan was at work, but I called to see if he would meet me for lunch. I didn't tell him where I would be, but I gave him an address, telling him where to go. I knew that he was due in court at two o'clock, so I had to make this quick. I stood close by the door, looking out and waiting for him to arrive. Minutes later, I saw him park his car; then he got out. A smile came across my face. I couldn't ignore how handsome and well put together my man was. His tailored suits always looked spectacular on him, and I don't think there was ever a time when his hair wasn't trimmed and his shoes didn't shine. I was one lucky woman. He seemed to be the man of my dreams. I hoped and prayed that what I assumed wasn't true; and if it was, I didn't know what I would do.

The second I opened the door for him, his masculine cologne hit me. I could have fucked him right then and there, but with all of the sales associates lurking around, that wouldn't have been a good idea.

"Hello, sweetheart," I said, greeting him. "Thanks for coming. I wanted you to give me your opinion on three dresses I have in mind for our wedding day. I know you're not supposed to see what I'll be wearing, but these dresses are similar to what I really want. Do you think you can help me?"

Jonathan looked around at the bridal shop then smiled at one of the associates who stood nearby, waiting to assist me.

"I, uh, don't mind helping out, but I didn't know that we set an official date yet," he said.

"We haven't, but I think we should do so soon. I'm excited about spending the rest of my life with you, and you will have yourself a beautiful, loving, and dedicated wife real soon."

"I'm looking forward to it." He looked at his watch then reached for my hand. "Come on and show me the dresses. I don't have much time, but if my opinion matters, I don't mind offering it."

I escorted Jonathan to a sitting area that was surrounded by mirrors. While he took a seat on one of the leather couches, I went into the spacious dressing room with the associate, who helped me ease into the first dress I had chosen. It had a plunging neckline that revealed a sliver of my cleavage. Pearls were tightened at the waist, and the satin material hugged my tiny curves. The dress was more than beautiful. If this marriage thing actually worked out, I would surely find something similar to this one.

"Oh my God," the associate said with a wide smile on her face. "You look amazing. He is going to be so pleased with this, and you are going to be a stunning bride."

Of course that's what she would say. I did look good, though, so I took her word for it. She opened the door for me to walk out, but unfortunately for me, Jonathan was no longer on the couch. He stood close to the counter with his cell phone up to his ear. Another associate tapped his shoulder, and when she pointed in my direction, he turned around. His eyes grew wide and his conversation came to a halt. I saw him take a swallow and then he cleared his throat.

"I will be there as soon as I can," he rushed to say. "Don't say anything until I get there. I don't want you to blow this."

Jonathan eased the phone into his pocket and continued to stare at me. I held out my hands then shrugged my shoulders.

"Well, what do you think? Do you like this one?"

With his hands in his pockets, he strutted my way. The other women looked on with jealousy in their eyes. He appeared to be all the man any woman could hope for. I so wished that our little world was perfect. Deep down, I knew that it wasn't. *Damn Sylvia.* Her timing was off.

"I'm almost speechless," he said with a serious look on his face. "I don't like it, baby, I love it. That is the dress you need to wear. I don't want to see you in anything else on our special day but that dress. You are killing it."

His words made me smile. "Are you sure? You haven't seen the other ones. They are just as beautiful."

"No. I don't care about the other ones, and I really don't want to see them. I love that one. It's you all the way. Turn around."

I turned to display my backside. I heard Jonathan take a deep breath then release it. "With all of these women standing around, I can't express how I really feel about the dress. Remind me to tell you later, but, for now, you need to get it bagged up and be done with your search."

This certainly didn't sound like a man who had been cheating on me. Maybe I had been barking up the wrong tree. Had I been wrong about him and Sylvia? Was he still deeply in love with me, and was marriage still on the table? It surely seemed like it was. If he was putting on a front, he was a damn good actor.

I rushed into the dressing room then came back with two other dresses to show him. He thoroughly observed the dresses but didn't change his mind.

"The one you have on is my final choice. I haven't seen you in the other ones, but I can already tell that they won't look as good on you as that one does."

"Okay. If you say so, I believe you. Thanks for your opinion, and just so you know, the one you chose just happens to be the most expensive one. You're not going to be upset with me for spending this kind of money on a wedding dress, are you?"

"No. I don't care how much the dress costs, and you can show up at our wedding naked for all I care. All I care about is you being my wife. That's all that matters."

My eyes welled with tears. I felt like an idiot for not trusting Jonathan. Whatever was going on, I guessed it didn't have much to do with Sylvia. I felt relieved. He told me to meet him outside, and after I took off the dress, I told the sales associate that I would be back later.

"Are you going to purchase it today?" She grabbed my arm as I started to walk away. "If not, I'll be happy to put it aside for you."

I frowned and snatched my arm away from her. "I haven't made my final decision yet, but I appreciate your help. Thank you."

"You're welcome, but I really think you should buy this dress today. He wants you to have it, and if you don't put it on hold, I'm afraid that someone else will get it."

I hated pushy salespeople, and it upset me that she was about to ruin my day. "For the last time, Miss Pushy, I said I would be back later. Whether that means today, tomorrow, next month, or next year, I will be back. Thank you again, and have a great day."

The bushy-browed bimbo stood with her eyes bugged and her hand on her chest, as if I had offended her. I rolled my eyes at her then walked away. Once I was outside, I saw Jonathan leaning against his car. He was back on his cell phone, but he asked the caller to hold.

"Listen, baby, I need to get back to the office and pick up some things before I go to court. I'll see you at home tonight, and I will do my best not to be too late. Thanks for inviting me to come here. I love you, and I want you to give me a date for our wedding real soon."

"I love you too," was all I could say.

I gave him a kiss then told him that we would finish our discussion later. Jonathan sped off, and I couldn't help but to think how foolish I had been. I was now convinced that he hadn't been cheating on me. Shame on me for thinking such a thing. My insecurities had gotten the best of me. I had to admit that Sylvia was a beautiful woman, so the competition was steep. Nonetheless, Jonathan was in love with me. He proved that time and time again. I was so glad that I hadn't accused him of anything, and how stupid would that have been. The way I saw it, I was so damn lucky to have him.

CHAPTER 7

SYLVIA

I was looking forward to lunch with Jonathan on Thursday, but when I went to his office, his secretary told me he was out for the day. He could have called to tell me that. I was a little disappointed that he hadn't.

Instead, I went to lunch by myself. I decided to grab a bite at Friday's, and as soon as I walked through the door, I got the shock of my life. Dana was sitting at the bar, next to a white man. He was very attractive and quickly put me in the mindset of Daniel Craig. I was hoping that she wouldn't see me, but with the bar being close by the door, that was near impossible. She narrowed her eyes and her mouth dropped open. She whispered something to the man next to her; he turned around to look at me. He nodded and a fake smile followed. Dana patted his back, and with a skinny-leg pantsuit on, she tucked her purse underneath her arm then headed my way. From a distance, I saw the huge diamond ring on her finger glistening. She looked as if she was made of money, and her caramel skin was polished with tanning lotion. Her sandy brown hair was full of loose curls that hung several inches past her shoulders. It didn't appear that she had gained any weight, and as far as I could see, she appeared to be the same ol' bourgie Dana.

Pretending as if she was so elated to see me, she approached me with a wide smile on her face. She air-kissed my cheeks then stepped back to search me up and down.

"Girrrl, you look fabulous. I didn't know you were in St. Louis," she said. "Are you visiting or what?"

"I'm here for good. Atlanta was only temporary." My response was flat.

"Uh, okay. But come this way. I want you to meet someone."

For whatever reason, I followed Dana. Being in her presence made me quite uncomfortable, especially since our friendship had ended on a sour note. In the moment, though, I was being just as fake as she was. I could sense that she really wasn't feeling me, and I definitely wasn't feeling her. She swung around with the phoniest grin I had ever seen and then introduced me to Jeff Wilcox, her husband.

"Nice to meet you." He stood and shook my hand. "I've heard so many things about you."

It wasn't the first time I'd heard that statement. It wouldn't be the last. I guess I was the subject of plenty of people's conversations.

"Same here," I said, waving as if I were in a rush. "Take care. It was good seeing the both of you."

I hurried to move away from Dana and her husband. She reached for my arm to stop me.

"Really, Sylvia? I haven't seen or talked to you in years. What's with the attitude? Are you still upset with me? If so, for what? If I recall, you were the one who stole my husband away from me. Not the other way around."

I almost lost it. She didn't just go there, did she? Then again, I expected her to. Drama was her middle name. That's why I was eager to get away from her.

"I think I told you this before, but let me remind you of something. If I took your husband, that means he was never yours. What I recall is you cheated on him with a younger man, basically throwing Jonathan into my arms." I looked at her fine-ass husband. "It is my wish that Dana doesn't slip up again. If she does, you just never know what kind of woman will be watching and waiting to get her hands on you."

Neither of them had much else to say, but Jeff had a smirk on his face that implied my comment pleased him. Dana shook her head, appearing disgusted with me. Before she opened her mouth to say one word, I turned and headed toward the door to leave. I could hear her heels clacking against the hardwood floors. She followed me out of the restaurant, and that's when I swung around, coming face to face with her again.

"Look, Dana. I don't have no beef with you, okay? Things have changed, and it is my hope that we've moved on from a situation that left many of us hurt. It seems that you're happy with who you're with, and, just like with Jonathan, I'm sure your new husband is providing you with all of the money you can spend and credit cards you need."

Catching me off guard, Dana lifted her hand, delivering a weak smack. It was enough to jerk my head to the side; there was no question I was in disbelief.

"How dare you stand there and insult me, after betraying our friendship as you did? Bitch, you need to be bowing down to me and asking for forgiveness. Instead, you're treating me as if I was the one who backstabbed you. As if I was the one who lied to you and fucked your husband over and over and over again. Don't you have any remorse? Are you seriously that foolish where you think your actions were justified? Wake the hell up, Sylvia. The next time you see me, treat me as if you have some gotdamn respect."

I was in a different place right now, one that wouldn't allow me to slap this heifer back and beat her ass for putting her hands on me. Instead, I got her where it hurt, before walking away.

"Respect? Please. And don't speak about me and Jonathan as if our relationship is a thing of the past. We're still going strong. So strong that I'll send you an invitation to the wedding, as soon as it's in the works. Meanwhile, have a nice life and keep your husband close. He's gorgeous, and you already know how I am."

I turned to walk away. Dana laughed, continuing to lash out at me.

"Watch your back, trick! His fiancée, Lesa, won't stand for your games! She's a force to be reckoned with, and this time, you will pay with your life!"

I was so upset about what had happened, but Dana's threats went in one ear, out the other. She was lucky that her weak-ass slap didn't hurt. Nonetheless, I couldn't get focused on work back at the office, so I gathered my things to go home. Crissy had been out all week. She told me I could work from home for a few days if I wanted to, so I took advantage of her offer.

Later that evening, I found myself bored as ever. There was a time when I could call Jonathan to come keep me company. We'd watch movies, play cards, cook, basically have a ball. But I wasn't sure if inviting him to come over was what I wanted to do. I wanted him to chase me, instead of me always reaching out to him. I didn't want to come off as desperate. And the last thing I wanted him to know was my desire to have him in my presence at all times. I wanted so badly to be his wife. There was a possibility that it could still happen, so I remained wishful.

Friday was here before I knew it. I decided to go into the office and play catch-up, since I didn't get anything done from home. I wondered if Jonathan was at the office too. It was confirmed when I saw his BMW parked in his reserved spot. I hadn't planned on telling him about Dana; however, when I stopped by his office to say hello, he mentioned the contents of a note that was on his windshield.

"It's been on my mind ever since," he said, standing by the window and looking out. "I don't know who would do something like that, and I can't really say if the letter was intended for me."

Of course it was. And I had a feeling I knew who was responsible.

"I'm glad you mentioned the letter, because I have to tell you about an incident between Dana and me. I saw her and the hubby at a restaurant yesterday. At first, she seemed very chummy, but then she started cursing me and rehashing certain things from the past. She followed me outside and slapped me across my face when I refused to listen to her foolishness. As I walked away, she told me to watch my back because Lesa wouldn't stand for none of this. She also said something like I would pay with my life if I continued to see you."

Jonathan appeared stunned by what I'd told him, but like always, he defended her. "I can't believe she put her hands on you. That doesn't sound like something Dana would do, and she, of all people, has no reason to interfere in my life."

I cocked my head back. "Are you calling me a liar?"

"No, I'm not calling you a liar. It just makes no sense that she would be the one who wrote the note. Did you tell her the two of us were involved again?"

I wanted to lie but decided against it. "Yes, I mentioned something like that to her. She threw everything at me but the kitchen sink. I had to somehow fire back at her with a little truth."

It was apparent that Jonathan didn't like my answer. He eased over to his chair then released a deep sigh. "Damn, Sylvia. I wish you wouldn't have told her anything. What we do is none of her business. As a matter of fact, it's nobody's business. This is how shit travels from one person to the next. It won't be long before it gets back to Lesa. I don't want her to know about us; after all, she is the one I want to marry. If you keep running your mouth, you'll put me in a position where I'll have some explaining to do. Are you trying to ruin things for me, and have you told anyone else about us? I mean, like Crissy or some of the people who work here? You know how nosy the people around here are, and they're always looking for some kind of dirt on me."

I was taken aback by this conversation. All the hell he cared about was this getting back to Lesa. *Fuck Lesa.* I was so upset that I didn't bother to respond. All I did was roll my eyes at Jonathan, and then I walked out. He didn't come after me, and by the time I got back to my desk, I was fuming. I could barely get anything done, and I continued to escape into a daze every time I attempted to type.

I kept thinking that I needed to back off and stop pursuing him so much. Deep down, I knew that I needed to distance myself from him, but it was so hard for me to do. Hard because I could tell he was holding back on me because of Lesa. I wanted him to come to his senses and realize that she wasn't the one for him—I was. Marrying her would be a big mistake. But maybe I thought that way because I was the one in l-o-v-e, and love often made people think and do some crazy things sometimes. I understood that all too well, and I recognized that I was allowing Jonathan to have his cake and eat it, too. In the past, that was a no-no, but this time around I didn't want to come off as the angry, bitter bitch who fussed about every little thing he did and said. I'd lost him by being that way before, and if I had to bite my tongue and walk away from arguments, that's what I'd do. I was still worried about losing myself again, and I didn't know how much hurt I'd be able handle this time around.

It was my wish that things got better between us, and, by five o'clock, things were looking up.

He stopped at my desk and made an attempt to correct himself. Some of my anger had ceased by now, but I was still slightly on edge, so my facial expression was flat.

"Listen, Sylvia," he said, off to a good start. His soft tone got my attention. "I didn't mean to upset you earlier, I would really like for you to keep this things between us on the down low. That's all I ask. I don't think that's asking for much. Do you?"

My eyes narrowed as I gazed at him. I pressed my finger against my lips then winked. "Secret lovers we shall be. Whatever you want, Jonathan. Your secrets are always safe with me."

My sarcasm didn't work for him. He encouraged me to have a nice evening, and as he walked away, I turned my head to watch him. I truly felt as if we were traveling backward. I didn't want to go that route, but I also knew that it would take a little time, effort, and a whole lot of patience on my part to get him back on my team.

CHAPTER 8

JONATHAN

There was a time when it bothered the hell out of me if I didn't hear from Sylvia. She always made me feel as if I was the one who was wrong. If I apologized to her, she refused to accept my apology. That angered me in the past, but now I didn't care. I wasn't as concerned about her feelings as I was about Lesa finding out about us. I had to keep this a secret, and after our day at the bridal shop, I realized just how devastated Lesa would be if she knew what was transpiring behind her back.

We had a serious conversation that night, and I realized that hurting her would only cause me to hurt myself. We discussed a date for our wedding, but nothing was set in stone yet. Lesa mentioned three months from now; then she said she wanted to wait until next year. That way, all of her fashion shows would be over and she could plan to have the wedding she really wanted. I was down for whatever. The delay gave me more time to get my shit together and do my best to deal with this situation with Sylvia. It was hard to let go, and I kept telling myself that I didn't need her. I couldn't even explain why I kept finding myself between her legs. The pussy was good, but damn. I couldn't let that shit control me, and I had to start making more sense of my life and focus more on my future with Lesa.

In addition to that, Dana was on my mind, too. I hadn't spoken to her in about six months. I knew how to reach her if I wanted to talk, so I called to find out more about the situation between her and Sylvia. I also wanted to know if she was behind the note on my windshield.

"What is it, Mr. Ex?" she said over the phone. "I should've known you'd call."

Mr. Ex had been my name for the past few years. She pretended to be happy that we parted ways. I wasn't so sure.

"I had to call. I heard some ugly things about you. I wanted to reach out just in case the individual you put your hands on wants to press charges."

"Oh, please. Sylvia needs to get over herself. I can't believe she's over there whining about a measly, little ol' slap."

"So, you did slap her?"

"I'm not telling you a thing. You're probably defending her, and calling me so I can confess."

"I wouldn't set you up like that, but I do question your actions. Why are you still harping on the past? Tell me, and then explain why you left a note on my car." I was fishing. I figured Dana would tell me if she did.

"Jonathan, if I could, I would reach into this phone and slap some sense into you, too. I am over the past. What the two of you did was dirty, but I've moved on. I am happily married to a wonderful, rich man who loves me dearly. I love him too, and I'll be damned if I allow you or Sylvia to ruin my happiness."

"That's fine and dandy, but why did you slap her? That wasn't necessary, was it?"

"For me, it was. I just happened to see her the other day, and she's the one who confirmed that she's still lying on her back for you. She admitted to having no regrets for destroying our marriage, and, for the life of me, I don't understand why you've gotten yourself involved with her again. Lesa seems like a wonderful woman who doesn't deserve this. Women like her always get hurt, but they also get even. I reminded Sylvia of that, so hopefully she's paying attention."

"You said all of that to say what? That you were the one who put the note on my windshield?"

"What freaking note are you talking about? I don't even know what kind of car you're driving these days, and quite frankly, Jonathan, I really don't give a damn. Now, if you don't mind, I don't have time to discuss anything else. I'm in the fitting room with this gorgeous dress on, and the mean mug on my face isn't making my dress look good. Good-bye, Mr. Ex. Don't call me again unless it's really, really important. Anything involving Sylvia isn't."

Dana hung up on me. I just had to make sure that she wasn't the one who had written the note, so that only left one other person responsible: Lesa. Was it possible that she knew more than what I thought she knew? Was all this talk about setting a wedding date just for her to find out where my head was? Something was off, and if she had anything to do with the note, it was time for her to come clean.

I waited for Lesa to come home. She didn't arrive until one in the morning. It never angered me when she came in late, only because I knew what a hard worker she was. I was always able to reach her. We had spoken at least four times tonight. She advised me that she would be home after one. To her surprise, this time breakfast was on me.

She entered the house through the garage. I stood in the kitchen wearing nothing but my skin. Two plates were on the granite-topped island with omelets on them. Our orange juice was spiked with vodka, and a red rose was next to her plate. The kitchen was dim, and a few vanilla-scented candles gave off light.

"Surprise, surprise," she said after putting her briefcase on the floor. "You've been on a roll lately. What did I do to deserve this?"

"I wouldn't say that I've been on a roll, but just so you know, I'm willing to do whatever it takes to please you."

Lesa smiled. We sealed a lengthy kiss before taking our plates and drinks over to the table.

"I wasn't sure if you would be hungry, but I figured you hadn't eaten anything."

"I've been so busy today that I haven't had a chance to think about food. The next fashion show is in three weeks. I have my work cut out for me. Some of the outfits I made aren't quite coming together. Whenever you get a chance, I want you to take a look at them and tell me what you think."

"Let me look at them right now. I'm not sleepy, and all I have is time on my hands for the next few hours."

"Now is not a good time. If you think I'm going to come in here and ignore what you've presented to me and not take advantage of it, you're crazy."

I laughed as Lesa pushed the plate aside and stood to remove her dress. We hadn't attempted to go there again ever since our last unfortunate situation when I couldn't get it up.

"You're not going to have any problems tonight, are you?"

She eased closer to me. I grabbed her waist then pulled her to me.

"I hope not. And from the way things are look-ing and feeling down there, it doesn't appear that we will have any problems."

Lesa reached for my hard meat and began to stroke it, while I took soft bites and pecks against the side of her neck. One of my hands massaged her breasts, and my other hand squeezed her firm, sweet little ass. I was more than ready to dive into what I hadn't explored since my festivities with Sylvia. I was still hyped when we made our way over to the couch in the den. Things changed, however, after two or three strokes. Lesa's legs were high on my shoulders and her pussy had just locked on me. The warm, tight feeling aroused me for a minute or two, but my dick slithered out of her fast then deflated.

She felt it right away. Her closed eyes shot open, and disappointment was written on her face again.

"What is wrong with you?" she said through gritted teeth. "Damn it, Jonathan, what is going on?"

I didn't appreciate her tone. I tried to understand why she was upset, but this was embarrassing for me too. "There is nothing seriously wrong with me. I just can't stay hard all of a sudden. I'm not giving up, so lie back, take a deep breath, and relax."

Lesa took a deep breath then lay back. She really didn't seem into this, and her lack of enthusiasm didn't help me one bit. It pissed her off when I attempted to force a soft dick inside of her that wasn't working. Her pussy was dripping wet. There was no secret that I had let her down.

"Forget it, Jonathan," she said then sighed. "This is a waste of time."

I ignored her. It wasn't a waste of time. I wasn't about to save a wet pussy like this for another day. I did what any man in his right mind would do and used my tongue to perform for me. Lesa thoroughly enjoyed that, and as my tongue traveled deep to tickle her insides, she formed a high arch in her back and screamed.

"Now, that's what I'm talking about! Do that shit, baby. Go deep and maaaaake meeee commme!"

I gave it all I had. Sucked her until she was dry as the desert. Massaged her breasts until my hands got tired. Kissed her until our lips felt numb. She seemed satisfied. While we were now cuddled in bed, in our bedroom, I asked how satisfied she was.

"I'm okay, Jonathan," she said while laying her head against my chest. "It's just that this has never happened before. I don't know if it's because you're at the age where things like that can happen or if something else is going on. If I knew, it would make me feel a whole lot better. I hate to bring this up, but please tell me if there is something going on between you and Sylvia. I was sensing something very wrong, but then again, this relationship between us feels so right."

Her words caused my whole body to stiffen. I had to pretend as if I didn't know what direction she was coming from. And sometimes a man had to lie in order to protect his woman's feelings. "I can assure you that Sylvia has nothing to do with this. Why would you think that she does?"

"Because ever since she's been back in St. Louis, you've been a little different."

"Different? How? I don't understand why you feel as if I'm a different man."

"For one, you used to call me more often, throughout the day, to see how I'm doing. You've been going to the office more than usual, and you're taking a little extra time in the morning to get dressed. You've changed your cologne recently, and there are times when I see you in a daze, as if something heavy is on your mind. Not to mention the roses, the gift, and meals you cooked. I'm not saying you don't do nice things for me, but you've been going above and beyond for the past few weeks."

Women were too damn observant for me. I hadn't noticed any of this, but it made sense why she would call me out on it.

"Baby, you're fishing for something that isn't there. I may have changed up my routine a little, but that's because I've been feeling something different with you too. I think with Sylvia being back in St. Louis, you're worried about our future. If so, please don't be. I don't want you to feel uneasy about anything; that's why I've been going the extra mile to make sure you know how I feel about you. As for my issues with sex, I'm going to the doctor next week. I already set up an appointment so I can find out what's up."

"Great," she said, rubbing her feet against mine underneath the sheets. "I appreciate all that you do, but please know that you don't have to go the extra mile with material things to show me you care. I can feel what's in your heart, simply by your actions. Your phones calls, your 'I love you's,' your massages, your kindness, and your ability to make me feel comfortable when we're together satisfies me. You've been a little distant, though. I hope this change in you is nothing I should be worried about."

Lesa kept pushing. I continued to push back. I even asked her about the letter on my windshield, but I didn't tell her that it referred to me as a slick bastard.

"I believe someone put it on the wrong car," I said.

"Maybe so. People are always running around doing stupid stuff. If any woman has issues with her man, it would be wise to speak up and say so. I definitely would. That's why I need to know if you've been intimate with Sylvia."

Almost immediately, my body got tense again. I wasn't sure if Lesa felt it, but her ongoing questions made me uneasy. Lord knows I hated to lie, but I just didn't want to lose her. I felt as if we had built something that could be everlasting.

That's why I proposed to her. This thing with Sylvia was only a minor setback. I intended to deal with it and put closure to it real soon.

"No, I haven't been intimate with her. We're not in love with each other anymore."

"You may not be in love with her, but she is definitely in love with you. I saw it in her eyes. And if you haven't been intimate with her, have you kissed her?"

"No."

"Hugged?"

"No."

Lesa looked up at me, rolling her eyes. "Come on, Jonathan. I know you've at least hugged her."

"Yeah . . . yes, I have, but not like the kind of hugs that I give you."

To quickly change the subject, I gave Lesa a squeezing hug and kiss that put us in the mood again. My dick shot up but quickly went down. I told Lesa again I would get to the doctor soon. The truth was, I got to Sylvia sooner.

CHAPTER 9

SYLVIA

Jonathan took me back in time. We made love for hours, and as we sat in the tub, washing each other's backs, I was on cloud nine. My legs were wrapped around him in a tub filled with bubbles. This was just like old times. Jonathan couldn't deny how I made him feel.

"You sure do know what it takes to please a man," he admitted. "I thought I was losing my touch for a while, but it takes you to bring out the best in me."

I squeezed the wet towel on his chest and rubbed it. "Why did you think you were losing your touch? What made you say that?"

He shrugged and hesitated to answer.

"Tell me. What did you mean? Does it have anything to do with the note you found? Have you been getting more of them?"

"Nah, nothing like that. After speaking to Lesa and Dana, I've come to the conclusion that the note was for someone else. I was speaking about my sudden inability to perform. When I'm with you, I have no problem. With Lesa, it's a different story."

"What?" I wanted to laugh, but obviously this wasn't a laughing matter. "You're having sexual issues with your fiancée? How long has this been going on?"

"I hate that you asked, but it's been going on since we started hooking back up. I don't know what's happening to me. I told her I would go to the doctor."

"Please. You don't need a doctor. What you need to do is stop lying to yourself. Lesa isn't the woman for you and you know it. The woman for you is sitting in this tub with her legs wrapped around every inch of you and loving every minute of it. When you get real with yourself, not even a Viagra pill will save you."

Jonathan didn't respond. I knew what time it was, but he was the one who needed to face reality. The sooner, the better. I felt as if he really didn't want to talk about that subject, so I changed it.

"So, you talked to Dana, huh?" I said.

"Yeah, I called to see what was up with her. What a waste of time that was."

"I told you. She's an idiot. Leaving her was the best thing you ever did."

"I have to agree with that."

We laughed and continued to wash each other. I wanted Jonathan to spend the night, but I figured that he couldn't. We said our good-byes, and I watched as he walked down the hallway and pushed the button to open the elevator. He turned to me before getting on it.

"See you next week at work. Pick a day and time for lunch. It'll be on me. Until then, stay sexy."

He winked then got on the elevator. I was beaming and didn't close my door until he was out of sight. Feeling giddy as ever that night, I snuggled with my pillow, knowing that Lesa's days with my man were numbered.

Crissy was back in the office. She was acting like a real bitch. She got that way sometimes; all I did was stay out of her way. That didn't always work, simply because she always buzzed me to come into her office so she could tell me what was wrong.

"I am so freaking mad." She lit a cigarette then took several puffs from it.

"What's up? And just so you know, this place is a nonsmoking environment."

"To hell with this place. Ever since my dad died, Jonathan and Brennan have treated me like crap. Yes, I gave up my percentage of my dad's ownership, but when I changed my mind, I thought that the two of them would understand my passion for wanting to come back here and continue my dad's work. They act as if I'm incapable of doing anything. I just lost a freaking major client who wanted Jonathan instead of me to represent him."

"Well, Crissy, you know people are entitled to choose who they prefer to work with. And it's no big deal if someone wants to work with Jonathan or Brennan, is it? You all get paid a certain percentage regardless, so I don't see what the big fuss is."

Crissy whistled smoke into the air then smashed the cigarette into an ashtray. "The big deal is my record speaks for itself. Over the past few years, I've only lost one case. One, Sylvia, and that's because the prosecutor and judge had something going on behind my damn back. I can't prove it, but I know for a fact they did."

"Yes, your record is stellar, but so is Jonathan's. He was here way before you came on the scene, and, as you know, your father and he put this firm together from scratch. He will always be considered one of the best, and many people prefer to have a lawyer with his experience and expertise. I think you're taking this too personal when you shouldn't."

She sighed then dropped back in her egg-shaped chair. "Maybe I am taking things too personal. But hear me when I say I will not be run over by anyone. We women have to stick together around here. All this ill treatment in the workplace needs to stop. I can't believe this country has an issue with equal pay for women, and, starting today, every freaking woman here is going to get a raise."

"I don't know how Jonathan and Brennan will feel about that, but good luck. As for me, I'll happily take my raise and call it a day."

Crissy smirked then picked up her phone. She buzzed Jonathan's office. When his secretary connected him, Crissy asked if he could come to her office.

"Not right now," he said, as if he didn't want to be bothered. "Within the hour, possibly."

Crissy looked at me and rolled her eyes. Jonathan was a little snooty. I was surprised by his tone.

"I'll be gone in an hour," Crissy snapped. "We need to speak as soon as you can."

"Soon as in within the hour. Need to take another call, so good-bye."

Jonathan hung up. Crissy gazed at me with madness in her eyes.

"See what I mean? I don't know what's been up with his attitude. He acts as if his shit doesn't stink. I'm fed up with the treatment around here."

"Listen. I think you're blowing this way out of proportion. Jonathan is a busy man, Crissy. And you can't be demanding a meeting with him without scheduling it."

"Like hell I can't." Her voice went up a notch. "He may operate that way with you, sweetheart, but he won't with me."

Just that fast, she touched a nerve. I crossed my arms and took my voice up a notch as well. "And what is that supposed to mean?"

She didn't back down. "It means that he may have to schedule appointments with you, but not with me. When I snap my finger, he needs to come. This is business, and business should always take priority over playtime."

I was flabbergasted, as she continued to rant and take jabs at my relationship with Jonathan. It was apparent that not much had changed with some folks in the Lou. They still had problems controlling their slick mouths.

"Playtime?" I said with my hand on my hip. "What in the hell is that? And just so you know, I don't have to schedule a darn thing with Jonathan. He's on my time; I'm not on his. So wherever you're getting your little information from, someone is being very incorrect."

Before I could say another word, I saw Crissy's eyes shift toward the door. When I turned around, Jonathan was standing in the doorway with the meanest mug I had ever seen on his face. He cut his eyes at me, and then looked past me to address Crissy.

"What is it?" he said in a sharp tone.

Crissy fired back. "I need for you to approve several pay increases for all of the hardworking women around here. It's something my father would have wanted, and I hope you don't have a problem with my request."

Jonathan's arrogance was on display. He knew that Crissy didn't have a damn thing coming because he owned more of this firm than anyone. "I have a huge problem with it, and any raises around here will be decided upon by me. I'm not feeling it right now, so unless you have something else we need to discuss, I'm out."

Crissy's eyes shifted to me. "Sylvia, please excuse us. Feel free to go home for the day. I need some privacy as I clear up a few things for Jonathan. Obviously, he doesn't seem to understand that when I want something, I get it."

Jonathan stepped farther inside and didn't even look at me. I walked past him and closed the door behind me. Almost immediately, I could hear him and Crissy going at it. I gave them all the privacy they needed and went home for the day.

The second I put the key in the door, I could tell something wasn't right. The door wasn't locked, and the whole place felt sweltering hot. I rushed to the thermostat, seeing that it had been raised to nearly ninety degrees. I clicked the heat off, and as I started to open some windows, I heard a bubbly sound coming from the kitchen. I wasn't sure what it was. I was almost afraid to go to the kitchen to check it out. I tiptoed on the hardwood floors, causing them to creak. As I poked my head in the kitchen, I saw an aluminum pot on the stove with water boiling to the top. The lid on top rattled, and as the hot water hit the flattop stove, it sizzled. I immediately thought about the movie *Fatal Attraction*. I wondered if there was some kind of animal boiling in the pot. My stomach was tight and my heart raced with each step that I took forward. With my cell phone in my shaky hand, I stood in front of the stove, ready to dial 911. But that's when I noticed a folded piece of paper on the counter that displayed the word OPEN on top. I snatched the paper and read the contents.

BITCH, SOMETHING STINKS IN HERE. I DID MY BEST TO CLEAN HOUSE.

Unsure of what that meant, I reached for a potholder then snatched the lid off the pot. Inside was an array of my panties and bras tied together. I hurried to turn off the stove, and knowing that someone had been in my bedroom, I rushed to it. It was trashed. My comforter was slashed, cotton was all over, and every single one of my drawers was open. Clothes were strewn around, my flat-screen TV was busted, and my curtains were snatched from the rod. The mirror to my dresser was cracked, and BITCH was scribbled on it with red lipstick. I covered my mouth, and in tears, I nervously dialed 911. In an instant, I changed my mind and ended the call. If I had to retaliate because of this, I didn't want the police getting involved. I quickly called Jonathan but got no answer. In a panic, I left a voicemail, asking him to call me back ASAP. Two minutes later, he did.

"What's so urgent?" he said.

"Someone trashed my apartment. I need you to come here and see this now. I also want you to give me Dana's number. She's the only one, aside from your girlfriend, who has a reason to do something like this. My money is on Dana, and I'm getting her to stop this madness today."

"Calm down, and tell me what you mean by trashed."

Jonathan's voice was flat. It didn't even seem as if he cared. I was too pissed, and where was the fucking urgency?

"I'm not going to calm down! What is her number, Jonathan?"

"I have no problem giving you her number, but please don't go out there and do anything stupid. It's not worth it, and there are other ways to deal with this. I'll be done in about two or three more hours. I'll stop by before I go home."

I was in disbelief. *Two or three more hours? What the fuck!* It was so apparent that Jonathan didn't care about me the way he used to. I didn't know why I kept hoping and praying that he would eventually come around and do the right thing. If the shoe were on the other foot, I would be there for him in a flash. He would have my full support and then some. This was totally ridiculous, but I refused to cuss him out for not wanting to come sooner.

"Don't bother to stop by, Jonathan. Whenever you get a chance, please text Dana's number to me. I will deal with this by myself."

I hung up on him, not knowing if he would text Dana's number to me or not. A few minutes later, he did. I called, but her husband answered the phone.

"Hi, I'm trying to reach Dana. Is she there?"

"Who's calling?"

"Deysha. I'm an old friend of hers from college. We found each other on Facebook, and she told me to contact her when I came to St. Louis. My plane touched down a few hours ago, and I was trying to catch up with her before things get too busy."

"Oh, I understand. She's not here right now. She's at the beauty salon, but I can tell you where it's located."

"Please do."

Her husband gave me the name and directions to the salon Dana was at. I locked my door, rushed to my car, and drove like a bat out of hell to get to my destination.

Forty-five minutes later, I arrived. Without a care in the world, I charged inside of the not-so-busy salon, expecting to find Dana. I spotted her sitting underneath a hairdryer, reading a magazine. This time, I caught her off guard as I snatched her by the hair and yanked her from underneath the dryer.

"Miss Stalker, we need to talk. Now!" I dragged Dana by her hair, pulling her across the floor.

"Bitch, are you crazy?" She scratched at my hands with her long nails and swung wildly at me. "You are done! So done!"

"Not as done as you are!"

Many looked on, but no one interfered. They were all too shocked. The mad look in my eyes brought about much fear. I tossed Dana outside, causing her to fall hard on the concrete pavement. I was sure she regretted wearing high heels today, along with a short skirt and thong.

"You slimy bitch!" She charged at me, but I shoved her so hard that she fell again. This time, to keep her in check, I slightly opened my purse and pretended to have a gun.

"If I have to use my gun on your ass, I will. I'm here to tell you to stay away from me and Jonathan. If you ever come to my place again and pull the shit that you did, I will hurt you. I will have you arrested for harassing me, and with your ex representing me, I can promise you jail time. I'm on my way to get a restraining order against you. You'd better abide by it or else."

Dana laughed. "You have lost your damn mind. That's what happens when you mess around with men like Jonathan: you can barely see or think straight. I don't know what the hell you're talking about, but just like I told him, you're barking up the wrong tree."

"Lies, lies, lies. I don't want to hear your lies!"

"I'm not lying! And if you keep this up, I won't be the one going to jail. You will. Why? Because I'll be represented by a man who has waaaay more power than Jonathan. He's called my husband, so you'd better think before you act again."

Dana got up slowly. She looked down at her bloody, scraped knees, shaking her head. That's when we heard sirens.

In less than two minutes, the police had me on the ground with handcuffs on. Several women from the salon explained what had happened. According to them, I was the aggressor. Dana gave her side of the story, and it wasn't long before I was arrested and thrown into the back seat of a police car. A mean mug covered my face, and as the car slowly drove away, I looked out the window, only to see a smug look on Dana's face. She was thrilled.

I regretted going after her. *Maybe I should have listened to Jonathan and approached this in a different way.* It was too late now. I had to deal with the repercussions. I was sure the outcome wouldn't be pretty. Nonetheless, I had calmed down and listened to the officer lecture me while at the police station.

"You shouldn't be out there behaving like a kid," he said as he fingerprinted me. "What were you thinking?"

All I could do was lower my head in shame. What had I gotten myself into? Why was I acting like this? I wasn't even sure if Dana was the one who had trashed my apartment, but somebody did. Possibly Lesa. I was sure that Jonathan wouldn't hear me out if I told him my thoughts about her. Maybe I'd get around to it, but for now, I was still hurt that he didn't drop everything to come see about me.

I guess I couldn't be too mad, huh? Remaining calm would be in my best interest. I had a cash-only bail of $10,000. He was the only person close to me with that kind of money, aside from Crissy. She had already done so much for me. I surely didn't want to bother her. I had to, though, because Jonathan didn't answer his phone. Yet again, she came through for me. Within the hour, she came to the police station to pick me up.

"They didn't hurt you or anything like that, did they?" she asked.

I looked at my scraped elbows from when I was wrestled to the ground. Other than that, the officer who arrested me wasn't too rough.

"No, I'm okay." I looked out the window as Crissy drove down the street. Jonathan hadn't even returned my phone call. By now, I had hoped to hear from him.

"Well, you don't seem okay. What's on your mind? Are you still upset with me from earlier? And please tell me exactly what happened to your apartment."

"I'm not upset with you, but I would like to know how you knew Jonathan and I were seeing each other again. As for the apartment, I want you to see for yourself what someone did."

"That's fine. And no one told me anything. There are cameras all around our offices, sweetheart, and you and Jonathan are busted. Lucky for you, I'm the only person, aside from security, who looks at the cameras often to see what's going on. That's how I knew you all were lovers again. I'm a little disappointed, because I really wanted you to move on with your life without him."

"I am moving on."

"With a man who is planning to marry someone else? Jonathan isn't the same man you were with years ago. He's changed. That's why he and I can't see eye to eye on anything these days. I respect the man, but to be truthful, he's an asshole."

"I guess that means we women in the work-place won't be getting raises anytime soon."

"No, it means that you won't be getting a raise anytime soon. The other women will."

I cocked my head back and crossed my arms. "Why's that? Was that his decision or yours?"

"Mine. I pay you too much already. You don't need a raise. The only thing you need is a decent man who loves you and only you. One who is honest, as well as respectful. A man who doesn't belong to anyone else and who can provide for you like no other person has."

"Please tell me where to find him, and I'll leave Jonathan alone."

Crissy laughed. "I'm still looking too. God help us."

Minutes later, we arrived at my apartment. Crissy was stunned by the looks of things, and she moved slowly around my bedroom with her mouth wide open. "You should have choked the life out of that hussy. Dana has always been a little wacky, but I'm not so sure about this Lesa chick either. I've only met her a few times. There's something about her that I don't like, and it has nothing to do with her being gorgeous."

I put my hand on my hip then pursed my lips. "Gorgeous? I don't think so. She is not cute—at all."

Crissy threw her hand back at me. "Oh my God. Yes, she is! Her figure is to die for. And of course you're going to say that because you're screwing her man."

"If I weren't screwing him, she'd still be unattractive to me. And exactly what figure are you talking about? She is as bony as it gets. Just flat all over. Jonathan doesn't have much to work with, and that's why he can't get it up."

Crissy covered her mouth and laughed. "Did he tell you that? Please tell me he didn't say that to you."

"It slipped one day, but I don't think it was his intention. Regardless, you need to redefine gorgeous. Please."

"You have your opinion; I have mine. The woman works out and it shows."

"Hell, I work out too. My body shows curves and sexiness that any man in his right mind would appreciate."

"For the record, you are gorgeous too, but let's give credit where it's due. Now, on another note, sweetie, what are we going to do about this little sticky situation? No one should be allowed to cook your drawers and get away with it. I say call the police to file a report, and then it's time for you to get a private investigator involved."

"Are you serious? Are they really able to find out what's up, or do they just charge people a fortune and take their money?"

"Over the years, I've worked with some of the best. I'll give this one I trust with my life a call tomorrow. Let's find out who's really behind this. That way, you don't have to keep going out there and beating people up."

"If you think a private investigator will help, I'm all for it. Take the money I'm supposed to get from my raise to pay him. That should cover it."

We laughed. I was so thankful for Crissy. She helped me clean up, and we drove to the store to get another TV and some curtains. I also purchased some new bra and panty sets. Afterward, we had dinner, but all throughout, I was hurt because Jonathan hadn't called to say one word.

CHAPTER 10

JONATHAN

Sylvia had to know that I was frustrated with her for running her mouth about our relationship. I asked her not to, but there she was, standing in Crissy's office, telling her things that weren't her business. I didn't know how to handle our relationship anymore. Shit was starting to spiral out of control. The incident at her apartment let me know that someone was angry and watching us. I couldn't put my finger on who it was, but I planned to hire someone to assist me in finding out what in the hell was going on.

In the meantime, I had spoken to the young man, Taye, who allegedly had drugs in his car. I didn't believe the officers' side of the story not one bit. They were wrong for trying to pin something on any young man, especially one who was smart and had a promising future ahead of him.

I shared my thoughts with Jaylin as we walked around a new home he was having built in one of the most elite and exclusive neighborhoods in Missouri. It was almost done, and I had never seen anything quite like it before. I questioned what he would do with a 25,000-square-foot home with two swimming pools, a twelve-car garage, three kitchens, a bowling alley, massive theater room, elevators, tennis courts, tree houses, and so much more. Obviously, money wasn't a concern for some people.

"What do you mean by what I'm going to do with it? Live, my brotha. Live and be happy," he said.

"It doesn't take all of this to live and be happy, does it? You got houses all over the damn place. When is enough, enough?"

"It's never enough, especially since I travel a lot. But St. Louis is home. I need to have a livable home here, because I visit here more than I do any other place. Besides, Nokea likes it here. So do the kids."

"Better than Florida? That place is nice too, but this right here is . . . There aren't too many words to describe this house."

"Change. We like change, and just when you think you got something good, something else comes along and you just gotta have it. This house has so many things that the one in Florida doesn't have. Wait until I show you this."

We walked to the other side of the house where Jaylin showed me his golf course, and a breathtaking view of the Missouri River. Numerous other castle-like mansions were down below. His house was at the very top.

"This is my world," he boasted. "I've worked very hard to be here. At the end of the day, we deserve this, and nothing pleases me more than to see the faces of others when I open those gates out there and park my car. I'm sure you know what I mean. It's a good feeling."

I had to agree with him. And even though this was a bit much for me, this house definitely suited him. We walked outside by the pool and sat in a lounging area. A stone bar was being built, and several construction workers were there to put on the finishing touches.

Jaylin rubbed his hands together then clenched them. "I want to thank you for taking this case for me. I wouldn't have asked you to do it if I didn't believe Taye was innocent. I don't know what in the hell has been going on with the cops around here, and it's unfortunate that many of us can't fight this shit without money. I love what the protestors are doing, and it's good to see so many young people involved. I'm hopeful that their efforts can and will make a change."

"I think they will too. I'm going to do everything in my power to prove his innocence and get those officers responsible fired. Possibly in jail, if I have enough evidence to prove what they did."

Jaylin reached out, slapping his hand against mine. "That's what's up. I knew I could count on you, and whatever you want, just let me know."

I looked around then laughed. "I want a got-damn house like this. That's what I want. Maybe a few horses and a white picket fence, securing acres and acres of nothing but land. Can you handle that?"

"Sounds like my place in Texas. The kids love it there too, but as for you, naw, I can't handle that. I can handle a new car for you, and it looks like you need one. That BMW done had it. How many women you been rocking in that back seat? It's getting old, and I'm sure they be real uncomfortable back there."

"Stop hating," I said, laughing. "I just got that last year. You know it's cold. So cold that I don't rock women in back seats anymore. The only woman I am rocking is Lesa. I'm sure you can't say the same about Nokea, or can you?"

Like always, he was straightforward. "No, honestly, I can't. We have a better understanding about our lives together, and no matter

who I'm rocking or who's rocking me, my lifetime bond with Nokea will never be broken. As
for you and Lesa, that's bullshit and you know
it. You mentioned that Sylvia is back in St.
Louis. There ain't no way in hell, Mr. Jonathan
Taylor, that you gon' sit there and try to convince me that you haven't hit that."

"I plead the Fifth, but it's not as serious as
it was the last time. I'm still bitter about her
opening up her legs to you, and that, to me, was
quite a surprise."

Jaylin didn't appear surprised at all. He
shrugged and blew it off. Sylvia could have had
sex with anyone but him. We'd had this competition thing going on for years, and I regretted
that he had the upper hand on this.

"Man, please. Sylvia couldn't resist, and trust
me when I say it will never, ever happen again.
She got a problem with looking in the mirror
and seeing who she really is. I despise people
who aren't willing to do that, and prefer to judge
others. Just watch your back with her. If you're
really down with Lesa, you may want to cease
your action with Sylvia. She doesn't do well with
rejection. I'm sure you already know this."

I replied with sarcasm. "I do know all about
her, but thanks for the advice. The plan is for
me and Lesa to get married soon, but there's

something about her that's holding me back, too. Unfortunately for me, I don't know if it's the guilt I'm feeling from messing around on her or there's actually something about her that is making me feel this way."

"Any woman cooking grits after six o'clock p.m. would concern me too. I haven't met Lesa yet, so allow me to meet her and check things out. I'm good at reading women. I can tell who's there for better or worse, only for the riches, or simply there for dick."

I thought about this for a minute then agreed to it. "Cool. Let's all have dinner tonight. You name the place and we'll be there."

To no surprise, Jaylin chose Morton's. I told him we would meet him at seven, and then I called Lesa when I got back to the office to make sure her schedule was clear.

"Sweetheart, you know I'm trying to get things together for the fashion show. Will your friend still be here next week?"

"No, he won't. He's leaving tomorrow. I really want you to meet him."

She sighed then replied, "Okay. But I'll have to meet you at the restaurant. I'll do my best not to be late."

"That's all I ask. Thank you."

"You're welcome. And by the way, have you seen your doctor yet? You told me you would, but you haven't said anything about it."

Yet again, I had to lie. I hadn't seen my doctor because my dick was only having issues with her. "I saw him, but all he did was give me some of those Viagra pills. Not sure if I want to take them, due to the side effects. There are minimal effects, but I'm a healthy man. I don't like to put anything inside of my body that may not be good for me."

"I understand that, but we have to do something. It's been a long time, Jonathan, and I miss the feel of you."

"Same here. We'll talk later. A client is waiting to see me."

Lesa said she'd see me later. I headed into the lobby to speak to one of my clients, who was frazzled about her upcoming court case. They were never easy, but in the end, I assured her that everything would be fine.

Hours later, Jaylin and I sat at Morton's, waiting for Lesa to come. We were both suited up, and there was no secret that we always tried to outdo each other. The competition had always been steep, only because Jaylin had good taste, just as I did.

"I guess the place you always go to must have had a two-for-one sale," he said, looking at my banker striped suit that was designed to fit my frame only. His chambray blue linen suit was nice, too, but this time, I had the edge.

"I don't do two-for-one sales unless it pertains to my cereal. I'll leave that to you and Shane. By the way, how is your partner in crime doing?"

"Somewhat happily married, still working with me, and he has another baby on the way. You should give him a holler. He asked about you when I told him I was coming to the Lou."

"What does he want to discuss? I know Frick still handles most of his legal matters, too, doesn't he?"

"Frick is my attorney, not his. Shane trusts you. I do too, but you already know that Frick and I have known each other for a long time. Ever since I was sixteen."

"I understand that level of trust. But you do know that I'm here for you and Shane, if ever needed."

Jaylin nodded then stroked his goatee as he glanced at his watch. It was almost eight o'clock. Lesa hadn't shown up yet. Quite frankly, I was a little embarrassed.

"Is she always late like this?" he asked.

"Not really, but when we spoke earlier, she said she might be late."

Jaylin didn't respond, but deep down, I knew he felt what I did. There was little to no excuse for this. If the shoe were on the other foot, I would have canceled my plans and rushed to meet one of her friends. I was just about to call her, when I looked up and saw a waiter escorting her our way.

"Here she comes," I said, standing then buttoning my suit jacket.

Jaylin stood too, and when Lesa reached the table, his hand was already extended to hers.

"Lesa, right?" he said. She nodded and smiled like the Cheshire cat. Her eyes were wide, and she took a hard swallow before releasing his hand.

"Yes, Lesa. That's my name."

"I'm Jaylin. Jaylin Rogers. Nice to finally meet you. Please, have a seat."

I pulled the chair back, but before Lesa took a seat, she leaned in to give me a kiss. "So sorry I'm late. I couldn't get out of there for nothing in the world. Finally, I put the clothes on hangers and told everybody that I had to go."

"No problem," I said. "I'm glad you made it."

Right then, the waiter walked over to the table. He poured our wine and started a quick conversation with Jaylin. I watched Lesa from across the table. She seemed real nervous about something. Her eyes shifted from him to me. When she looked at me, she displayed a fake smile. I smiled back, but, to be honest, her appearance disappointed me. Her hair looked dry and thirsty for moisturizer. It was as if she hadn't put forth any effort to look decent. I told her where dinner would be, and for her to walk in here with a sundress on and flat sandals, I wasn't pleased. Normally, she dressed down at work, but there had to be enough time for her to go home and change into something more elegant. Something sexy or classy would have done the trick, too. After looking around at the numerous businesslike people in the room, and at a few Cardinals players who came in, I assumed she felt like crap. Maybe that's why she was nervous. She kept raking her hair with her fingers and swooping her hair behind her ears. Even her makeup looked different, and her skin looked awfully pale.

She leaned in to whisper to me, "Do you know where the restroom is? I need to go freshen up a bit."

The second I stood to pull her chair back, her cell phone rang. She looked to see who the caller was but didn't bother to answer. I assumed that the call wasn't important, so I nudged my head toward the ladies' room in the far corner.

"Over there," I said.

"Okay. Be right back."

She looked flustered as hell. I wasn't sure what was up with her tonight, and I made a mental note to inquire about it when we got home.

Jaylin and I conversed with the waiter about the Rams' future in St. Louis. Many people were upset because there was a possibility that the Rams would go back to L.A. It was the talk of the town, and it didn't appear that anyone could stop it from happening.

"I think it's unfair," the waiter said. "But what can we do?"

"Not a damn thing," Jaylin said. "Money talks and bullshit walks."

We all agreed. The waiter said he would be back with more wine, and when he walked away, Jaylin looked at me.

"Where did Lesa go?" he asked.

"She went to the restroom to freshen up. So, what do you think?"

"I'll give you my overall opinion later, but for starters, not bad. She's cute, a little thin for my taste, but nonetheless pretty. Pretty late, too."

Maybe I was being too hard on Lesa about her appearance, but it was important for my woman to look her best when I introduced her for the first time to my boys. It was just something that men always appreciated. A part of me felt real let down because I knew Lesa could do better.

A few minutes later, she returned to the table. Her phone rang again, but she ignored it. I wondered who had been bugging her this evening, and when I suggested that it might be important, she waved me off.

"If it were important, I would answer. You know the people I work with like to bug me about every little thing. They don't think I have a life. I already told them, when I'm with my man, do not bother me."

At times, the ringing of her phone was rather annoying. She never turned it off, and it would sometimes ring in the middle of the night. It seemed as if the people she worked with couldn't do anything without her, and they often contacted her for advice. There was definitely a time and place for everything, though. Now wasn't the time, simply because I wanted to enjoy dinner with her and Jaylin.

I had already ordered for Lesa while she was in the restroom. The waiter said it would be several more minutes before the food came. Meanwhile, we sipped wine and talked as if our lives hadn't missed a beat. Jaylin listened in as Lesa told him about her fashion design career.

"Very impressive," he said. "I would love to see some of your pieces. I'm always looking for something exquisite to purchase for my wife. She loves clothes. She also has a boutique that sells clothes made by up-and-coming designers. The two of you should hook up."

"I would love that. Jonathan said you were leaving tomorrow. Is there a way for me to reach you? I would love to show you some of the pieces I created for the fashion show, and—"

For the third time tonight, Lesa was interrupted by the ringing of her cell phone. Once again, she looked to see who it was but ignored the call. I wanted her to answer, but even more than that, I wanted her to turn the phone off. I didn't dare say anything to her about how irritated I was, only because she never complained about my ongoing calls. During dinner, and out of respect for other people, I often turned off my phone or put it on vibrate so there would be no interruptions. If only she would do the same.

"As I was saying," she continued, "Jaylin, you and I need to talk."

"To be honest," he said, "you may have better luck with my wife. I'm not into the fashion business, but she definitely is."

"I'll be happy to speak to her, but are you sure she's your wife? I didn't notice a ring on your finger."

Jaylin looked at me then lightly touched his goatee. "Married men don't always wear rings. But trust me when I say that she's the one you should speak to."

Lesa winced and seemed as if she'd caught an attitude. "I think all married men should wear their wedding rings. That way, women won't get misled. When Jonathan and I get married, wearing our rings will be a must. If he refuses to, then we basically have no marriage."

She touched my hand and smiled. I had no problem wearing my ring, but I knew why Jaylin wasn't wearing his.

"That's your and Jonathan's preference," Jaylin said. "And, ring or no ring, many women don't care. My wife knows that there are plenty of women who go after what they want, and a ring won't stop them."

"That's sad. I have to agree with you on that. I hate those kinds of women, and the men who give in to them are scumbags."

Lesa sipped from the flute glass, waiting for Jaylin to respond. He responded by looking over at me; then he glanced at his watch.

"What time do you want to meet tomorrow?" he said to me. "My plane leaves at three, so we need to wrap up things before then."

"Meet me at my office around eleven. That should give you plenty of time."

Jaylin stood then straightened his suit jacket. "I won't be able to stay for dinner, but it's on me. I'll see you tomorrow, and it was nice meeting you, Lesa. Take care of John-John, and I'll be sure to get your info and pass it on to my wife."

Lesa quickly reached into her purse then pulled out a business card. She passed it to Jaylin, and he removed it from her hand. "Give that to her," she said. "And it was nice meeting you too."

Jaylin nodded then made his way to the door. She observed him as he stopped to chat with a few people and started talking to another waiter. Lust could have been in her eyes, but she also seemed annoyed by him. I wasn't sure, but her concentration was broken when her cell phone rang again.

"Who is that calling you?" I said, annoyed my damn self.

"One of the models, Princess. She's always bugging me like that. I'm seriously about to tell her that I do not want her to be included in the show. I don't like it when people keep harassing me about things. If I don't answer my phone, obviously that means I'm busy."

I wasn't buying it, but I didn't want to go there with her, considering what I was doing behind closed doors. I was just glad when the food finally came. We enjoyed a delicious meal and good conversation. That was until I inquired about her thoughts of Jaylin.

"He seems like a well-educated, arrogant man who cheats on his so-called wife. I truly don't believe he's married, and isn't he the one who you said Sylvia had sex with?"

Sometimes, I talked too much. But since she put it out there, I answered her question. "Yep, he's the one. And he and his wife have been together for a long time. I've never met a couple where love runs that deep. I hope that we stay together as long as they have."

Lesa shrugged. "Whatever works for them. But no woman should be okay with her man not wearing his ring."

"Even if she doesn't wear hers?"

"I wonder why. Like I said, I don't believe he's married, but if he is, I assure you their way of thinking won't work for us. And in reference to your ex-girlfriend giving up the goodies to him, she's a tramp. Her going after him doesn't surprise me. Women like her get all hot and bothered when they see a nice-looking man like him. The first thing they want to do is take off their panties and let him have at it. But, knowing her, she did it to hurt you. Does it sting, Jonathan? I mean, how do you feel about her having sex with a man like him?"

Her words caused me to frown. "What do you mean when you say a man like him? He's like any other man, as far as I'm concerned."

"Uhhh, not. I mean, I can see why she would be attracted to him. He's got that little swag thing going on, and his money can be smelled from miles away. Many women are drawn to that, especially simple bitches like Sylvia, who only want a wet coochie and nothing else."

Lesa was putting it on thick. For starters, I guessed she'd forgotten that she was willing to give up the panties the first day I'd met her, too. They officially came off a week later, so she didn't have much room to talk about Sylvia. If I hadn't been sitting here tonight, she probably would have jumped over this table to get at Jaylin. I saw through her tonight, and, to be honest, I didn't like the way she was starting to represent herself. After two years together, maybe I didn't know enough about her.

"To say I wasn't disturbed by Sylvia's actions would be incorrect. I was. But I realized a long time ago that I can't control what people do. All I can do is control me, myself, and I. My relationship with Sylvia was over during that time. If she felt a need to hook up with him, so be it."

I left it right there and quickly changed the subject. The subject was her upcoming fashion show and her trip to New York. That conversation took up much time, and we didn't leave Morton's until almost midnight.

I was tired as hell the next morning, but since I told Jaylin to meet me at the office, I got up around nine and went to work. By eleven, he was at my door, ready to provide his thoughts about Lesa.

He held out his hand and started to count down on his fingers. "Slick, sneaky, cheating, psycho, evil, and pretty."

"What?" I shouted.

"You asked my opinion and I told you. That is not the sweet, charming woman you've been speaking to me about. I hope you're not planning to marry her anytime soon. I am highly disappointed in you, John-John, for not being able to figure out the good ones from the bad ones."

"I think you're wrong about her, man. She had a long day yesterday, and she wasn't prepared to meet you. With that being said, I'm not saying she's perfect. I have a few concerns too, but for the most part, she's as good as it gets."

"It's a bad sign when you have to start making excuses for someone." He took a seat then leaned in to my desk. "First of all, her appearance, meaning her choice of clothes, didn't bother me one bit. She didn't have to get all dolled up to meet me. The fact that she was late pissed me off, and I didn't buy her excuse. Her hair was flat in the back, meaning that she had been somewhere lying on it. Her dress was wrinkled, and she was not wearing a bra or panties. I could smell sex from across the table, and when a person starts talking about who or what they hate, I have a problem with that. *Hate* is a strong word. It represents evilness, and that's what I took from our conversation."

"This makes no—"

Jaylin lifted his hand. "Hold up a minute. I'm not done. You asked for my opinion, so hear me out. You have the law thing on lock, and I have the relationship thing going for me. She took issue with me not wearing a ring. As a matter of fact, she noticed. And when I suggested that she reach out to Nokea, she wanted to discuss things with me. I'm the one with the business card, and I would put some money on it that if I called her right now, she'd make herself available. By the end of the day, she wouldn't even remember your name."

"Jaylin, come on, man. Don't be so full of yourself. Not every woman desires to be with you."

"You're absolutely correct. They don't, but I know for a fact that she would go there in a heartbeat. I know her kind, John-John. Seen it too many times before. You'd better be careful with her. If she finds out about this thing you got going on with Sylvia, she's going to lose it!"

I immediately thought about the note, and about what had happened at Sylvia's place. I hadn't told Jaylin about those incidents, but when I did, he jumped up from the chair.

"I told you!" he shouted and darted his finger at me. "Man, you are going to wake up with a knife in your back. Maybe yo' ass may not wake up at all. I did not get good vibes from her, as I never did with Dana. Sylvia . . . I got my problems with her, too, but she gives good head, so I'ma be nice. She ain't psycho either."

"You didn't have to go there, you know? And please eliminate all that talk about you and Sylvia. Let's get back to Lesa."

"Don't take it personal. We both were drunk. Lesa, however, is psycho. Did you or did you not hear how many times her phone went off last night? We are both businesspeople, and we know that business calls start to subside after eight. Sex calls start rolling in after that.

Her phone kept ringing like a lover was trying to reach her. Her eyes got real shifty when she looked at her cell phone, and she kept looking out of the corner of her eye to see if you were watching. I'm shocked that you haven't been on to her."

"I'm still not convinced that she knows what's been going on with me and Sylvia. If she did, I know she would confront me. Wouldn't a so-called psychotic woman confront me? You know damn well she would, and she wouldn't be able to contain herself."

"Like hell. She's plotting and planning, man. Waiting for the right time to take you down. You gotta beat her to it. Start paying attention and stop working so damn much. That's your problem. You work too much and you never have time to really evaluate and observe the women in your life. You're so damn eager to get married again, and I don't understand why."

"Family values. My parents are representing, and I want to follow suit. I want what they have, but I have to admit that time is running out for me. I'm getting old. Also, I've been going about things the wrong way. My career is, indeed, everything. Most women aren't down with that."

"Some are, some not. And I'm not one to preach to you about marriage; after all, it is a beautiful thing. But with it or without it, you should first make sure that the woman in your life is in your corner and that she's not up to no good."

I got up to go pour me a shot of Hennessy. Offered Jaylin some, but he rejected it. "Rémy only. Thanks, but no thanks."

"Don't get me wrong, Jaylin, I get what you're saying, but I can't expect to have a woman fully in my corner if I'm not completely in hers. Thing is, I can't be upset with Lesa for creeping if I've been doing the same thing too."

"But what if she was creeping before you? What if she has a dark side that you don't know about? All I want you to do is your homework. If it all checks out, and I'm completely wrong about this, I will shave all of my hair off and go bald for the next two years. I'm that confident that Lesa has skeletons."

I stood in deep thought while gazing out of the window. Yes, I had some homework to do. It was time for Lesa and me to have a conversation I didn't want to have. I had to come clean about my interaction with Sylvia. I didn't want anyone to get hurt, and if Lesa was as off as Jaylin claimed she was, I had to do something now. I turned my head to look at him, but wound up looking past him at Sylvia, who opened the door and stood in my doorway. She didn't look too happy. I guessed she was upset because I hadn't spoken to her since her apartment had been trashed. And with Jaylin in my office, it seemed as if the day was about to take a turn for the worse.

CHAPTER 11

SYLVIA

I was sickened about Jonathan not reaching out to me after the incident at my apartment. It was on my agenda to let him have it, but then apologize and ask him to clear up this little mess with me being arrested. But when I rushed into his office, I got the shock of my life. My number one enemy was there, leaving me speechless.

After our Hell House experience, I was sure Jaylin wasn't happy to see me either. The blank expression on his face said so, and the way he looked at me with those steel gray eyes let me know that all was not forgiven. Regardless, the sight of him always did something unusual to my body. My pussy was trying to travel back down memory lane, as if it wanted to feel him again. I hurried to shut down that feeling by looking past him and at Jonathan who didn't appear happy to see me either. The two of them must've been arguing or something, because no smiles were coming from either one.

Jonathan spoke up first. "I guess I don't have to introduce you to Jaylin, Sylvia," he said. "It's obvious that you already know him well, as he does you."

Talk about disrespect. *Really?* I couldn't believe he had gone there, and I didn't care what was troubling him. He had no right to put it out there like that, as if I didn't mean shit to him.

"Yeah, we do know each other," Jaylin said with his hands in his pockets. "How are you doing these days, Sylvia? Good, I hope."

"Shut the hell up talking to me, Jaylin." I was blunt and wasn't about to pretend that I liked him. "You know darn well that you couldn't care less about how I'm doing. Don't stand your egotistical tail there and pretend like you do."

Jonathan's eyes grew wide. Even he was shocked by my words. He wasn't aware that the only other man who could set me off like this was Jaylin Rogers. I never told Jonathan about the ugly way Hell House ended. It wasn't good.

Jaylin replied with a smirk on his face. "I'm surprised by your nasty words, Sylvia. I seriously thought that you would take a little time out to reflect and take in all of the advice that was given to you, but I guess that some people never really grow up. Some people stay in the same fucked-up situations and keep on making the same damn mistakes. It's sad to know that you haven't made much progress. I can only hope that Jonathan wakes up and rids himself of ignorant women like you. You're a waste of time, and I refuse to waste another breath schooling you." He swung around and looked at Jonathan. "Remember what I said. See you again in a few months. Let me know how the case goes with Taye."

We evil-eyed each other as he walked past me and out the door. If I had a bat, I would have used it to whack his ass a few times. Instead, I walked farther into the office. Jonathan spoke up before I did.

"What was that all about?" he asked.

"I don't even want to talk about it. What I would like to discuss is you. Why haven't you called to check on me? You know what happened, and I can't believe you haven't even called. You act as if you really don't care about me anymore. I'm starting to feel as if this has all been a waste of time. Then, you stand there and allow Jaylin to speak to me as he wishes. Your so-called introduction was insulting and totally unnecessary."

Jonathan sat on the corner of his desk, wringing his hands. "Okay," he said. "You deserve to know the truth, so here it is. I'm not in love with you anymore, Sylvia. I enjoy our time together, but I have no plans to take things to the next level. I don't call because I don't feel like talking or hearing you gripe all the time. I don't stop by because I don't want to see you. And while I'm deeply concerned about what happened to your apartment, you were the one who decided to take matters into your own hands. I hope that worked out for you. As for my introduction to Jaylin, what else was I supposed to say? You fucked my friend, and I can't forgive you for that. I will never forgive you, and I just can't see myself being married to a woman who had his dick in her mouth."

Well, damn! My face had fallen to the floor and cracked into a thousand and one tiny pieces. My heart sank to my stomach. My body felt as if it had melted and my feet were like stones. I couldn't move; didn't want to breathe. His words hurt. Truthful or not, they hurt. Hurt so bad that I had no response. Regrettably, he kept going.

"It's time to grow up, Sylvia. We're getting too old for this shit, and these petty arguments should be behind us. We've done it all from A to Z. Had ups and downs and all arounds. From boardroom arguments to courtroom arguments, I've had enough. I'm starting to feel as if you like this kind of shit, but, just so you know, I'm done."

What, a fucking break-up? I mean, he was really going all out to get me where it hurt. I couldn't let him get away with this; and, childish or not, a response was needed.

I answered when I walked up to him and slapped the shit out of him. His head jerked to the side, and when I attempted to slap him again, he grabbed my wrist and squeezed it. I snatched it away from him and spoke through gritted teeth. Tears were trapped in my eyes. I did my best to force them back.

"I don't even know where to start, but I guess right here. Your ass wants me to grow up, but you're the one still running around here playing games with two women and lying about your feelings. You, Jonathan Tyrese Taylor, talk a good damn game, but the truth is your game has been played before. I figured you were using me, and it is my wish that Lesa finds out about us and hangs you out to dry. I can't wait for that day to come. When it does, don't you dare crawl back to me for forgiveness. Good luck to you and your future bride. Go live happily ever after and tell her I said she's got herself a real fucking winner."

Jonathan sat with his arms folded, eyes narrowed, and a blank expression on his face. Just for showing that he didn't give a damn, I smacked his ass one last good time. I then marched out of his office with tears still trapped in my eyes. I kept blinking fast to clear them. By the time I reached the staircase, I let it all come out. I cried uncontrollably. Clenched my chest because it hurt. Pounded my fists against my legs because I was mad. Mad at myself for falling back into this trap again. Disgusted that I had allowed him to treat me this way. Frustrated that I couldn't get it right and was highly disappointed by my choices. I broke down like I had never done before. Hung on to the rail so I wouldn't fall, but wound up falling to my knees. Prayed for God to give me strength, but was so sure that He wouldn't come through for someone like me. Maybe it was time for me to face reality. A while back, I thought I did. My reality was that I was still in love with Jonathan, but now I knew that he didn't love me. He never really did, even while he was going through ups and downs with Dana. I was convenient. All I'd ever been to him was convenient. *Damn. Damn. Damn.* Realizing the truth made this hurt even more.

CHAPTER 12

JONATHAN

One woman down, another one to go. It was never my intention to hurt Sylvia, but the truth was what she needed to hear. The sexual encounter between her and Jaylin affected me more than I was willing to admit. I couldn't handle it, and every time I saw him, it made me think about how badly Sylvia had dissed me. Therefore, it was time for us to move on. I felt relieved in a sense, but not fully relieved because I had to confess to my wrongdoings and hope that Lesa would do some confessing too.

Instead of going home, I drove to a studio that Lesa and some of the other designers rented. I could hear talking and laughter inside. The door was open, so I went inside and saw numerous models standing around and several people who appeared to be there to assist. I spotted Lesa in the far back of the room. A tall female model was standing in front of her while getting fitted for a dress. Lesa had a pen in her mouth and her legs were crossed. Her hair was in a rough-looking ponytail, and she was dressed in a balloon-like jumper with large pockets on it. I didn't want to interrupt her, but if I didn't, I was sure she would be here all night.

I headed her way, saying hello to several individuals who had spoken to me. Lesa looked up and seemed surprised to see me. She removed the pen from her mouth then displayed a smile. We embraced, and as I held her tightly, she sucked in a heap of air.

"You smell so good," she said, complimenting me. "Did I buy that cologne for you?"

"I'm not sure. You probably did, especially since you're always taking care of me."

"Yes, always. What brings you here?"

"I thought we could go somewhere in private and talk. Saw my doctor again today, and I wanted to tell you what he said." I had to say that, just so she would be willing to stop what she was doing and find a private place for us to talk.

"Jonathan, is everything okay? By looking in your eyes, I'm worried."

I nudged my head toward the exit door. "Let's go talk."

"There aren't many private places around here. Why don't I gather my things and meet you at home in about thirty minutes. That would be better."

"Sounds good." I kissed her cheek. "See you at home."

After saying good-bye to the others, I went home and waited patiently for her to come.

I sat in my office, thinking about how I was going to break the news to Lesa. I felt terrible for creeping behind her back, and I wondered how she was going to react to all of this. I kept thinking that my timing was off, that maybe I should wait, but as I pondered more about it, I came to the conclusion that she needed to know the truth. She didn't deserve this, and it was up to me to tell her what was really going on, before she heard it from someone else.

I lifted my head and watched the clock on the wall tick away. I could have prevented all of this had I kept my eyes on the prize and told Sylvia that we couldn't undo the past. I didn't know why I just didn't say that to her, especially since I had a woman like Lesa in my life. No matter what happened tonight, my intentions were to still be with her. I just needed to get this out in the open, and I wanted to give her an opportunity to express herself as well. I was optimistic that once we both put our cards on the table, everything would be okay.

While examining how the night would unfold, I went to the kitchen to get a shot of vodka. I tilted the glass to my lips then opened my mouth wide to toss the shot down my throat. It burned, so I pounded my chest then cleared my throat. I reached for a cigar then made my way into the great room to wait for Lesa.

She arrived almost thirty minutes later. I was still sitting in the great room, puffing on a cigar. I had changed into casual clothing and comfortable house shoes. Lesa gave me a hug then slowly sat back on the couch to join me.

"Wha . . . what did the doctor say?" she said with fear in her eyes.

I got straight to the point. "I haven't seen the doctor, but I knew that if I didn't tell you that, you wouldn't have felt the urgency for us to have this conversation. All I know is this: things are changing between us. I will own up to my reason for causing this change, but I want you to fess up too. There is nothing more pitiful than being in a relationship where you know you've been lied to. Where you feel uncomfortable, and feel as if there is no trust. I know you feel that way. Rightfully so."

She interrupted me. "I don't know how I feel about the trust thing, but I have felt uncomfortable lately."

"Don't you think I know this? After all, you said it yourself: I've changed. The truth is, I have. The reason?" I paused, just to read Lesa for a few seconds. She was definitely tuned in and her eyes were so bugged that they looked as if they were going to break from the sockets. Her hand slightly trembled and her foot kept patting the floor. I could tell she feared the worst, but I had to shut down the lies, deceit, and betrayal.

"The reason is I've been having sex with Sylvia. I know it was wrong, but I felt a need to go there with her again, just to see if something was still there. My feelings, however, are not the same. I told her that today, and I also let her know that I'd been, basically, using her."

Slow tears ran from Lesa's face. Then they sped up. She smacked them away, and her lips quivered as she began to speak. "I . . . I knew you had been sleeping with her again. Damn it, Jonathan, I knew it! That's why you couldn't perform for me. You made me feel as if I wasn't good enough, when all along you were fucking her. Now you want me to believe it's over? Really?"

"It is over. I'm telling you this because I know it's over. I want you to stop with the notes, and how you ever got into her apartment to trash it, I will never know. You don't have to do that, baby. You don't have to chase after me to find out what I've been up to. Now you know the deal. I've come clean and I feel horrible. I will do whatever it takes to make this up to you."

Lesa's face twisted. She cocked her head back and shouted at me, "What are you talking about? I didn't trash her apartment. I don't even know where the bitch lives, but I will definitely go confront her after this. I knew she couldn't wait to get her hands on you again. When you told me she was coming back to St. Louis, I suspected that this shit would happen!"

I wasn't sure if I believed Lesa, but I didn't want to push. Her cries started to get louder and she covered her face with both hands. "I trusted you, Jonathan. I trusted that you would do right by me. I gave you everything I could give. Please tell me, where in the hell did I go wrong?"

I moved closer, attempting to put my arms around her. She pushed me away. "Don't touch me," she screamed, causing my ears to ring. "Just answer my got-damn question. Where did I go wrong?"

"This was on me. I want you to be honest about some things too. Have you been seeing someone too? And, forgive me, but I don't believe you about the note and Sylvia's apartment. Who else could have done it? Why would anyone else care about my relationship with Sylvia?"

She snatched her hands away from her face. Snot ran from her nose and over her lips. Her face was a pinkish red and her eyes were near swollen. I wanted to console her, but she didn't want me near her right now.

"I don't know who else could have done that. Probably someone else you've been sticking your lame dick into. I can't believe you have the audacity to sit there and ask me to come clean about my indiscretions. I don't have any, Jonathan, but I'll tell you this: I wish like hell that I would've given myself to Lance when he approached me about sex. I've definitely been deprived, but I was able to shake off his advances. I wish I would have taken him up on his numerous offers for dinners, movies, trips, getaways, but noooo. I declined. I did so because I thought we had something special. I thought you loved me, and I thought you would be able to shake off women like Sylvia, who would only do us harm. But you didn't. You didn't, Jonathan, and I can't spend another day in this house with you."

This was not how I wanted things to turn out. I suspected that she would have some skeletons too, but from the looks of it, she didn't have much. All of that stuff Jaylin mentioned earlier was in my head. I didn't see a psychotic woman before me. I didn't see one who had cheated, nor did I see one who was trying to be slick. I saw a hurt woman. One who had nothing to do with what had happened at Sylvia's place. One who had faith in me, in our relationship. I had let her down.

Without saying another word, she rushed off the couch and went into our bedroom. While remaining calm, she gathered some of her clothes from the walk-in closets and stuffed them in a suitcase. I watched but didn't try to stop her. There was not much for me to say, other than, "I'm sorry."

"I'm sorry too. I'll be back for the rest of my things this week."

Lesa dragged the heavy suitcase to the door. I followed her with sadness covering my face. She turned at the door and lifted her hand. In one pull, she snatched off her ring then tossed it to me.

"No need for this," she said. "Give it to Sylvia. I'm sure it fits her finger better than mine."

Saying no more, Lesa walked out. This was another failed relationship that left me feeling awful. I had a feeling that I had fucked up this time, but while Lesa was so sure that it was over, I wasn't. I intended to fight hard at getting her back.

there would be no more us, and I totally regretted giving myself to Jaylin. In doing so, it was
apparent that Jonathan had lost every ounce of
respect for me.

I was sitting at my desk, biting a nail. When
I looked up, I saw Crissy staggering down the
hallway, looking as if she'd had too much to
drink. Her eyes were starting to show bags,
and she wasn't as jazzy as she had been before.
I wanted to find out what was going on with
her, but I was so caught up in my mess with
Jonathan that I didn't have time to inject more
drama. Crissy's life was full of it, and her problems never seemed as big as mine. With all of
the money she had, all she had to do was take
a long vacation and seek the peace she needed.
Then again, as a friend I felt bad for not always
making myself available to listen to her. All she
wanted to do was vent, and the least I could do
was listen. She was the only real friend I had,
and, quite frankly, the only person I trusted.

She stopped at my desk then set her Michael
Kors purse on top of it. "I have a super long day
ahead of me, but you and I need to discuss what
to do with your assault case. I know it has been
on your mind, and I've already sought out an
attorney for you who can help. You mentioned
Jonathan, but I don't know if that's a good move.

I could defend you, too, but with us being close friends, that could be a problem."

"I understand that, and please scrap Jonathan. I don't want nor do I need his help. I would love to sit down and talk to any attorney you recommend."

"That's great. His name is Ben Clayton. I'll get him on the phone to see if he can talk to you this week. The sooner you get this over with, the better. And to be honest with you, Sylvia, this case is going to be a little difficult to try. You won't walk away without any consequences. There are several witnesses who saw you attack Dana. You don't have much of a defense, and we can't prove that she trashed your apartment. If I had to predict the outcome, I'd say you may be looking at jail time, a hefty fine, or probation. Could be two of the three or just one. Not sure yet."

Hearing her talk about jail time scared the hell out of me. I was a hothead sometimes, and many times I couldn't control my actions. I reminded Crissy that Dana had slapped me a week before the incident at the salon. It didn't seem fair that I had to pay for what I'd done to her, and nothing would happen to her.

"We will address all of that. It may make a difference, and I want you to tell Ben everything.

This is going to be costly, so I will front you the money. Somehow or someway, you must pay it back."

I wasn't a freeloading friend. I intended to pay Crissy back every single dime that she put out on my behalf. "No worries. I can't thank you enough. You have no idea what your support and friendship means to me."

Crissy reached out to give me a hug; then she removed her purse along with several folders from my desk.

"Hey," I said, looking at her tired eyes. "Are you okay? You've been so consumed with what's been going on with me, and I'm concerned about you. You don't look well."

She threw her hand back at me, as if it were no big deal. "I'm as good as I'm going to get. Been working my ass off, and I barely have time for me anymore. I need a long vacation. Looking forward to my trip to Dubai later this year, but I may go somewhere else sooner. I get tired of coming to this place every day, but I love what I do. The money motivates me, too."

"Well, you certainly have plenty of it." I laughed. "But, on another note, if you need anything from me, let me know. I'm here for you too."

"I know you are, and thanks for being such a good friend. I have a meeting scheduled for this morning, but I should be free for lunch. Will you join me?"

"Of course I will. Just let me know when you're ready."

Crissy walked to her door then turned around. "Oh, I almost forgot." She snapped her fingers. "I spoke to the private investigator the other day. He has a few questions for you, and then he said he'd get on seeing what Miss Lesa and Dana have been up to. One of them is about to get busted."

After all that had happened, I wasn't interested in what Lesa or Dana was doing. This was one last thing I didn't have to worry about. "Girl, forget it. I'll have to tell you why later, but there's no need to waste his time."

She frowned and didn't seem to like my answer. "What? Are you sure? I mean, don't you want to find out which one of them is responsible for trashing your apartment? We need to find out who the culprit is so we can turn their little world upside down."

"Like I said, it doesn't matter. Besides, I bought me a 9 millimeter that is going to rock somebody's world if they enter my apartment again. Trust me when I say they'll regret it."

Crissy laughed while shaking her head. "You are so bad, Sylvia. But I love it! Be careful with that thing, though, and be sure to stay within the law if or when you have to use it. We'll talk more at lunch, okay?"

I nodded and watched as she went into her office then closed the door. I, on the other hand, sat thinking about my unwanted departure from Jonathan. My thoughts were in and out, and before I knew it, I looked up, seeing that it was almost noon. Crissy had already left. I called her, and she told me to meet her at CJ's in fifteen minutes. I couldn't wait to eat and was starving.

Forty-five minutes later, I sat at CJ's with Crissy, stuffing my face with Buffalo wings and a salad. The food was delicious; I couldn't wait to tackle dessert.

"Slow down," Crissy said, dabbing her mouth with a crisp white napkin. "What's the rush? You won't get fired for taking an extended lunch, trust me."

I playfully licked Buffalo sauce from the tip of one finger. "I can't help myself. I haven't eaten this good in about three or four days. These wings are off the chain. You should try some."

Crissy cut her eyes at me then looked around at the crowded, noisy restaurant that served some of the best food in the area. Several waiters and waitresses moved quickly, trying to make sure each table got served. We looked at the table next to us, as an angry-looking man in a business suit complained about the size of his stuffed mushrooms.

"They're usually bigger than this. Find me some bigger ones or else I'll order something else."

I couldn't believe the arrogance of some folks. But with all of the uppity people in the restaurant, I was sure the staff knew how to handle them.

Crissy reached for one of my wings to taste it. She nodded then licked her finger too. "They are good, but you aren't pregnant, are you? Eating like that makes me nervous."

"No, I'm not pregnant. I thought I told you before that I couldn't have children."

"That's right. You did tell me. But what you haven't told me about is Jonathan. What happened between the two of you?"

I put the wings aside and started to tell Crissy about Jonathan's and my abrupt departure from each other. She kept dropping her mouth open and shaking her head. A few sips from her water followed, and her eyes kept rolling. She couldn't wait to chime in.

"I can't believe he treated you like that, but then again I can. How dare he? I told you that man has changed. He is not the man you knew years ago. Nonetheless, I want you to do me one huge favor."

"What's that?"

"Introduce me that hot-ass friend of his. I know you know who I'm talking about, and I don't blame you one bit for screwing that guy. If I could get one single hour with him, I would use my time wisely."

This time, I rolled my eyes at her. "I assume you're talking about Jaylin, right?"

"I don't know what the hell his name is, but when I saw him up close and personal, I just wanted to throw myself at him. Those eyes . . . There is something about his eyes that instantly drew me in. I recently saw him with Jonathan, and, from your description, I figured he was the one you screwed. He is the only one of Jonathan's friends you screwed, isn't he?"

I rolled my eyes even harder. "Whatever, Crissy. Save the dig for another time and forget about your little favor. I would never introduce you to Jaylin, so figure out something else to do with your hour. Besides, we're supposed to be friends. You wouldn't want my leftovers, would you?"

She pursed her lips then laughed. "When it comes to a man like that, a friendship can't be considered. All I want is the sex. On a scale from one to ten, I can look at him and tell he's a one hundred. But you tell me. Is he better than Jonathan?"

I was getting ready to answer Crissy, until I looked up and saw several tall, giddy women prance into CJ's. Some were extremely beautiful, causing several people in the restaurant to turn in their seats. Crissy's eyes were locked on them too, and we both were stunned to see Lesa walk in behind them. She looked out of place and was dressed in plain, baggy clothes. Her jeans hung low on her waist, and the oversized shirt she had on hung off her shoulder. It was short enough to expose her midriff. A cap was on her head, and loud pink lipstick covered those big lips. I still couldn't understand what Jonathan saw in her. I kept trying to figure it out, until Crissy poked at my arm.

"Stop looking," she whispered. "I told you she was gorgeous. I would die for that figure."

I cocked my head back, instead of pushing her out of the chair like I wanted to do. "Excuse me, but that heifer is too skinny. Your figure is better than hers, even though you bought it."

We teased each other a lot. That was just me returning the favor for her paying Lesa a compliment.

"I paid a fortune for this body, but I'm still not satisfied. I have an appointment with the surgeon next week. Unfortunately, I forgot what day and time. Damn it."

Crissy removed her cell phone from her purse. She started to search through her calendar. As she did that, I got back to my salad but kept taking peeks at Lesa and her crew. I guessed I must've been paying too much attention to them. She spotted me looking at her, and didn't hesitate to come my way. I removed my high heels from underneath the table, just in case she came over to pull a Dana on me. This time, I wasn't having it.

"Hello, Sylvia," she said while standing across from me. "I'm so glad I caught up with you. I had anticipated on reaching out to you, and this certainly saves me the trip."

"Catch up with me for what?" I said with an attitude. Crissy appeared shocked. Her eyes were wide and she wasn't sure what was about to happen.

"To let you know that Jonathan is all yours now. Since you couldn't keep your legs closed, and he couldn't control himself, I let him walk. No more marriage. No more anything." She wiggled her fingers so I could see that there was no ring on her finger.

"I'm not exactly saddened to hear your news, and, just so you know, I kept my legs closed. Jonathan was able to pry them open, so I let him have at it because he said you had issues with helping him get it up. Now, if you don't mind, I'm having lunch with my friend. We also don't want everyone in here to know our business, so go back to your seat and try me another time."

Lesa snickered, but I could tell her feelings were bruised. That changed when she hit me with something that I thought was between me and Jonathan.

"Yeah, I heard you were good when it comes to getting men up. You were able to get his friend up, too, and I listened in on a phone conversation one day where the two of them compared notes." She fanned herself and laughed. "Girl, what they said about you wasn't good. I knew then that Jonathan had lost all respect for you, and that you and he would never walk down any aisle. What I didn't expect was for him to have sex with you again. But a dog will always be a dog, especially when there are so many cutthroat women out here who don't give a hoot about the next woman."

"Boo hoo," Crissy interjected. "Didn't she tell you we were having lunch? Save the drama for your momma, honey, and scat. This conversation is over."

The people sitting next to us were all tuned in. They were waiting for me to reply, but I didn't say a word. Lesa walked away, giggling as if she had gotten something off her chest. I was shocked to learn that she knew about my involvement with Jonathan. *He must've told her.* I wondered how that conversation went, but I was not going to pick up the phone to call him.

Crissy leaned over close to me and whispered in my ear. "She rubbed me the wrong way, so let's get that bitch. To hell with Dana right now. I want some dirt on Lesa, and I wholeheartedly believe a private investigator can get it for us."

I was against it earlier, but now that Lesa decided to confront me as she had, I was all for it. I lifted my glass of water and Crissy lifted hers.

"Let's drink to bringing a bitch down," I said.

We clinked our glasses together then laughed. I looked forward to finding out what kind of woman Lesa really was.

CHAPTER 14

JONATHAN

When things felt as if they were falling apart, I turned to the one person who made me feel whole. The one person who meant everything in the world to me, and who made my days and nights seem brighter. Her voice had a way of calming me, and with so much on my mind, I needed to hear from my daughter, Britney. I had been calling her like crazy, and she finally called back. She left a long message, telling me she was okay and that school was going well. I hated that I missed her call, but I was in court. When I reached back out to her, I got voice mail.

"Glad you're doing well," I said. "I hope you're coming home soon, and be sure to call me back to let me know when you intend to. Love you, princess. And please, please, please be good."

I hung up then tossed my briefcase in the car. I hadn't spoken to Lesa in two days, but when I got home, I saw her car in the driveway.

The trunk was up. It looked as if she had been gathering more of her belongings. I parked my car, and as soon as I got out, she rushed out of the front door with several pieces of clothing draped over her arm. We stared at each other, but it wasn't long before she rolled her eyes and looked away. I walked up to her, blocking her from putting clothes into the trunk.

"That's how I get treated?" I said. "No hello or anything, huh?"

"Jonathan, move out of my way, please. I have nothing else to say to you."

"Why not? We can't even speak to each other anymore?"

"No. Besides, you do too much talking already. I can't believe you told Sylvia that I couldn't get you hard. Why would you put our business out there like that? I can only imagine what else you said to her."

My face twisted. *Guess I have another thing to thank Sylvia for.* Thoughts of the two of them conversing angered me, and I knew more had been said. I guessed Lesa decided to go confront Sylvia like she said she would. Unfortunately, I couldn't stop her.

"It wasn't like that," was all I could say. "I . . . I didn't tell her you were my problem."

"Right. You probably told her you had a problem and she was willing to fix it."

I released a deep sigh then pleaded with her. "Why don't you put the clothes down, chill, and let's go inside to discuss this. I really want us to work through this. I love you and I miss you like hell. Sylvia is not the woman I want a future with. My future is with you."

I waited for Lesa to respond, but all she did was slam her clothes in the trunk. She then rushed back inside to get more items from her closet. I walked inside, begging and pleading some more for her to give me another chance.

"Just one more chance. I made a mistake and I regret having sex with her. You have to be honest with yourself and realize that, aside from this incident, I've been a decent man to you. Not perfect, but definitely good enough. You can't deny that, can you?"

Lesa kept snatching her clothes from the hangers, trying to ignore me. When I moved forward to grab her waist, she jumped back. She pointed her finger at me, as anger swept across her face.

"All it takes is one time to fuck up, Jonathan. How can I be with a man I don't trust? How do I really know that it is over between you and Sylvia? If she's not around to help you get it up anymore, then what are you going to do?"

"I don't need her to help me get it up. I had some difficulties when I was with her too, so please know that this is not about you being unable to please me. The problem is with me."

I hated to lie, but I was willing to say anything to get her back. I didn't want her to feel as if I needed Sylvia. The reality was I didn't.

"I'm so ashamed of myself," I said. "I can't believe I hurt you like that. More than anything, I hurt myself. If I lose you, this would be one of the biggest mistakes of my life. Jus . . . just one more chance, Lesa. Allow me an opportunity to make you one of the happiest women in the world."

There was a long silence before Lesa pulled away from me. She walked into the bedroom then sat on the bed. "This can't be repaired overnight. I need time to think about this. Even though I know people aren't perfect, I still had a lot of faith in you, Jonathan. I had high hopes for us, and no words can express how disappointed I am." She paused then stood up. "I'm leaving. You'll hear from me in a few days. Please don't rush me to make a decision about our future. I can't say if I still want to be your wife, and, unfortunately, coming back to you means starting all over again. I don't know if I'm prepared to do that."

"Whatever it takes and whatever you want is fine with me. I will give you all the space you need, but please make a decision soon. I love you and I don't want to live much longer without you. This is our home. It hasn't felt like home since you've been away."

Lesa wiped her fallen tears. Without going back into the closet, she walked to the front door and opened it.

"I'll be in touch," she said then left.

I felt slightly better inside. I hated to see her cry, but I considered today progress. Now that the cat was out of the bag, there would be no more lies, no more betrayal, and possibly no more notes. I wondered if Lesa had been the one behind the note and Sylvia's apartment being trashed. I gave it more thought then scratched her name from the list. She just didn't have it in her.

To say that Crissy had been working my motherfucking nerves was an understatement. I didn't know what was up with her nasty attitude toward me and Brennan. Her numerous, ridiculous concerns were starting to work me. I had somewhat agreed to her request about giving the women around here raises, but I told her that it would be discussed further on my time, and when Brennan agreed to it as well. Unfortunately, he had a problem with the raises. We all stood in my office having a discussion that led to nowhere.

"The two of you are so full of it and bigheaded," she hissed. "I guess you guys think all women are good for is lying on their backs. When they do that, you all are so willing to dish out all kinds of money. I need those raises to happen pronto."

"It's so ridiculous and pathetic for you to go there," Brennan said. He was so upset that his face had turned red. His blond hair was messy from him raking his fingers through it, and he'd just about had it with Crissy too. Like me, he wanted her out of here. "Unless Jonathan agrees to it, no raises will happen on my watch. We have bigger fish to fry. The last time I checked our quarterly reports, we lost money. Now isn't the time to hand out raises."

"I have to agree with Brennan," I said. "Now isn't the time, but it is something I am willing to revisit in the near future."

Crissy's face tightened. She was so upset that she jumped up and stormed toward the door. "This is such bullshit. I just spoke to you, Jonathan, and you seemed on board with it.

Now, at the snap of your finger, you've changed your mind. I can't win with the two of you. I may as well fucking quit, like all of the other women around here should do."

I tried reasoning with her, but I assumed that this wasn't the real reason why she was so upset. Crissy was dealing with something else; she was possibly mad about me being in complete charge around here. That's simply the way it was after Mr. Duncan died, and there wasn't much that she could do about it. Other than that, I had no idea what could be troubling her. And, quite frankly, I didn't give a damn. I didn't have time to cater to a spoiled brat.

"I wish you would calm down." I tried reasoning with her. "I never said it wasn't going to happen. All I'm saying is it's not going to happen today. The other day, you forced me to give you an answer when I wasn't prepared to, but after looking over our yearly reports, as Brennan did, there is no question that we've lost money. Our accidental injury cases are down, so the priority should be trying to figure out ways to get more people to utilize our services again. If and when we see progress, hopefully soon, then we'll discuss raises."

To no surprise, Crissy didn't like what I had to say and walked out. Brennan shrugged, as if he didn't care either. Just as we started to talk, my secretary buzzed in to tell me there was a call waiting for me. I answered and it was Jaylin. I needed to speak to him, so I told Brennan that I would come to his office later so we could finish our conversation. After he left, I closed my door then put the phone on speaker.

"I'm already on it," I said in reference to the client he referred me to.

"Good. How are things going and what have you found out?"

"That two witnesses possibly recorded the incident with their phones. I'm doing my best to find out who they are. I should know something by the end of the week."

"Perfect. It would close this case shut and make those fools look like the racist mutha-fuckas they really are."

"Exactly. I hope those witnesses haven't deleted the videos. I question if they would be willing to share them. Sometimes, it's hard for people to speak up. In this case, I pray that they do the right thing. Taye is a decent young man. I would hate to see him put behind bars over something he didn't do."

"Me too. And shame on this fucked-up system and some police officers for not giving a damn."

I nodded, thinking about all that had been happening in St. Louis, as well as around the country. While I couldn't defend all black men who found themselves in this situation, this was one who I wasn't about to let go down for no reason at all.

"When is your next move to St. Louis?" I asked Jaylin.

"I'll be back at the end of the month. Need to come in and finalize everything with the house. It's coming together very well."

"I agree. And just so you know, things are coming together well over this way, too. Sylvia and I are done. Lesa and I, on the other hand, are working through some setbacks, but I think we'll be good too. With that being said, you need to prepare yourself to shave your head bald. You will also have to admit that you were wrong."

"Things may be good today, but it doesn't mean it will be that way tomorrow. I'm not hating or anything like that; you know it ain't my style. But Sylvia ain't your problem. Lesa will be. If you can't recognize the signs of a master manipulator, then I don't know what to tell you. In your line of work, you should be able to see through people like her."

"Master manipulator? I doubt that. But I'll keep you posted, because I've been thinking about how ridiculous you're going to look without your hair. It's laughable."

"Indeed, it is. But I would never make a serious bet like that unless I was sure about something. You, John-John, are in for a rude awakening. Peace, power, and prosperity. Holla soon."

We ended the call. I stared out the window, wondering if I was being naïve. There was a time when I felt the same way about Dana. I defended her until the end. Nobody could tell me anything about her. Then I learned that she had been cheating with a man who was much younger than I was. I was devastated. So hurt that it led me to the bedroom of her best friend. I surely hoped that history wouldn't repeat itself, excluding the best friend part because Sylvia and Lesa had no connection whatsoever.

CHAPTER 15

SYLVIA

For some women, it was easy to walk away from a man who made it clear that there was no room in his life for them. Then there were those who hoped and prayed that the relationship magically worked out, no matter how the man claimed he felt. I was one of those women. I couldn't accept the fact that Jonathan had moved on without me. Call me dumb, stupid, naïve . . . whatever. There was still a sliver of hope in me that we would be together.

My mind, however, was in another place today. I was worried about the outcome of my assault case. I had already been to see the attorney Crissy had recommended, Ben Clayton. I explained to him what had happened during both incidents with Dana. Basically, he told me that we could possibly settle this outside of court. I was waiting to hear back from him, but, thus far, nothing. So instead of staying cooped up in my apartment, I decided to go check out a movie. I thought about calling Crissy to see if she wanted to join me, but I changed my mind. I didn't want to hear any negativity today. All she would do was talk about work, and about how much she hated to work with Jonathan and Brennan. She complained a lot, and there were days when we couldn't get a single thing done at work because she kept going on and on. I was going through it too, so I didn't need the extra drama.

I slipped into a pair of jeans and a blue sweater. My heels provided a little more height, and the jewelry I wore enhanced my simple outfit. My freshly permed hair was parted through the middle and fell along the sides of my face. I moistened my lips with nude gloss then grabbed my keys and purse from the nightstand before leaving.

An hour later, I stood in line at the AMC theatre in St. Charles. The line was long, and I hoped that the movie I wanted to see wouldn't sell out. By the time I was able to purchase my ticket, it had. I was highly disappointed, only because I didn't want to go back home and torture myself while waiting to hear from Mr. Clayton.

I searched for other movie options, but nothing else interested me. Just as I got ready to walk away, a man beside me spoke up.

"The movie you want to see is sold out, right?" he said.

"Yes. I guess I was too late."

"I have another ticket. My daughter was supposed to join me tonight, but she just called and said that she couldn't make it. If you want the extra ticket, you're certainly welcome to it."

I was skeptical about taking the ticket. So many people were out here doing dirty things. I didn't know if he was up to no good and would snatch my purse as soon as I opened it to give him money for the ticket.

I took my chances, because I really wanted to see the movie. "If I take the ticket, I'll be more than happy to pay you for it."

"No. No problem. You'll actually be doing me a favor, because I don't want to be stuck with it."

I hesitated, but then I reached for the ticket. "Thank you. This is real nice of you."

"You're welcome. I'm going inside to get some popcorn. Would you like some too?"

"I would, but allow me to buy yours for you."

"No, that's okay. I have a coupon for a free bag of popcorn and soda. I want to use it before it expires."

I nodded then followed the man inside. While walking closely behind him, I checked him out from head to toe. He wasn't bad looking, but he surely was no Jonathan, who would never be caught using a coupon. The man wasn't as clean-cut as I liked my men to be, but his jeans and leather jacket looked nice on him. Body-wise, he had a little gut. It wasn't enough to turn me off, and I'd never dated a man who was bald. He looked to be in his late thirties, possibly early forties. He was chocolate, just as I preferred, and his facial hair was trimmed neatly. There was a diamond earring in his ear, and when I looked at his finger, he wasn't wearing a ring.

We stood in line to get our popcorn. That's when he kicked up a conversation.

"I hope you don't mind me sitting next to you. And before I forget, my name is Brian."

"I'm Sylvia. Of course I don't mind you sitting next to me. I appreciate you for giving me the ticket."

He used his coupon to pay for his things, but right after I ordered my stuff, he opened his wallet to satisfy the bill.

"No, really, I can't let you do that," I said.

"I just did and I insist."

I wasn't going to argue with the man. To be truthful, it had been a long time since I allowed someone to simply take care of me.

We walked next to each other, as if we were a couple. The theater was packed inside, and I was a little skeptical about sitting next to and conversing with a man I really didn't know. I didn't know if he would keep talking, annoying me, or if he would just sit and enjoy the movie like I wanted to. Minutes in, I had my answer. He was totally tuned in. The only thing I heard from him was laughter. The movie was great, and after it was over, I thanked him again for giving me a ticket.

"The pleasure was all mine. Sitting next to a beautiful woman wasn't so bad. I would love to see you again."

I don't know why, but I was reluctant to give him my number. He was somewhat attractive but wasn't really my type. I liked older, mature men with sexy bodies and impressive careers. I hadn't a clue what his occupation was, but getting to know someone else wasn't in my plans right now. I figured that since he had given me the ticket, plus paid for my snacks, it wouldn't hurt. I handed him my business card that included my cell phone number.

"I look forward to getting to know more about you," he said.

I forced a smile then replied, "Same here. Be careful out there. It's raining hard."

He looked at the rain coming down hard outside. "Shoot. My windshield wipers aren't working. I may have to stop and get some. But you be careful too. Talk to you soon."

Hmmm. Either too broke to buy windshield wipers or too lazy to put some new ones on. I wasn't sure which was the case. I hated to judge, but I paid attention to those things just so I wouldn't keep making the same mistakes with men.

My car was on the other side of the parking garage. I walked to it, thinking the comedy movie with Kevin Hart was hilarious. He surely had talent, and I looked forward to watching more movies with him in it. As I neared my car, I squinted. There was a long, deep scratch on the side of it. The scratch traveled from the front of my car to the rear of it. It didn't appear to be an accident, and I was furious that whoever hated me thought this was a bright idea.

I snatched my phone from my purse. The first person I called was Jonathan. Just like the last time, he acted as if he wasn't concerned.

"Who are you going to go beat up this time?" he said. "You may have pissed someone else off. I do not think Lesa or Dana is responsible."

If I were face-to-face with him, I would have slapped the shit out of him again. "You are so stupid, Jonathan. I don't know why you think the women you date are saints, and who else would keep doing stuff like this? I don't have any enemies, other than the tricks you've been with. If you care about them, you'd better do what you can to shut this mess down. Somebody is going to get hurt. If I had walked up on them, I would've used my gun to settle this, once and for all."

"Then you'd be in jail. I'm not saying that I don't care, but why are you calling me? They both said they didn't trash your apartment. Until I have some hard evidence, I don't know which way to turn."

"Are you working on getting some hard evidence? Of course not. You just believe everything they tell you. I bet you don't even believe my apartment was damaged. You probably think I'm making this up about my car, too, don't you? If so, I'll be happy to take pictures and show it to you."

"I never said I didn't believe you. What I'm saying is call the police. Report it, take pictures, and have some hard evidence. That's the only advice I can give a woman who found it necessary to tell my fiancée I couldn't get hard because she doesn't excite me. That was wrong on so many different levels, Sylvia, and I don't have much else to say."

I tightened my fist, wanting to punch something. Crissy was right. Jonathan had changed and it wasn't for the better.

"To hell with your fiancée. I'm sure she didn't tell you that she was the one who confronted me, did she? She said some things to me that got underneath my skin, but I'm not going there with you today. I have bigger fish to fry. Lesa is the least of my worries."

There was silence, and then he took our conversation in another direction. "We need to stop this, and there is no reason for us not to talk to each other as if we have some sense. How is your assault case coming along? Let me know if you need some assistance with it."

He was right. No matter how bad things were, this was unnecessary. "I think it's going along okay. Crissy introduced me to someone who can help me. I'm waiting to hear back from him. He went to court for me today."

"Okay. I hope it works out. I want you to know that I'm always rooting for you, regardless. I'm just in a place where I want to stay committed to the woman I'm with, without any distractions. With us, I felt like we kept repeating some of the same mistakes that we'd made in the past."

"I felt the same way too, but I was hoping for things to take a turn for the better. I'm not going to keep you. I need to call the police, but in the meantime, watch your back. Somebody doesn't like you, me, or both of us. If you discover who that may be, please let me know."

"You do the same. I handle so many court cases, and I'm starting to wonder if I have gained an enemy who's been watching me. I don't mean to scare you, but these things happen all the time."

"Trust me, I know they do. I'll let you know how the case goes, and thanks for the offer. If my attorney doesn't come through for me, I'll be searching for other alternatives."

Jonathan told me to keep in touch. After our call, I felt a little better. I calmed down and called the police. Within ten minutes, a police officer arrived to make a report. I inquired about possible cameras in the garage, but he claimed that there were none. I didn't believe him.

I returned home, seeing that I had missed a call from Mr. Clayton. He said that he had good news, and the good news was that I didn't have to face jail time. I was given probation for one year and was fined $5,000. The bail money could be used to cover my fine, but I didn't feel good because it was Crissy's money. Her money also paid for my attorney's fees. Somehow, I had to make this up to her. I called to share the good news with her.

"That's awesome," she said enthusiastically. "And I have some more good news for you. It's about Lesa. I'm on my way over there so I can tell you a little something I found out about her."

Even though I wanted to know, it was already late. If Crissy stopped by, I knew we would be up all night chitchatting. "Just tell me over the phone. I am so tired. I need to get some rest."

"Okay. I'll hold on to my information until morning. Let's meet at Forest Park so we can go walk away some of these pounds, too. Until then, I'll just say that you shouldn't be surprised. Jonathan really knows how to pick them."

I wanted to know what was up, but Crissy refused to tell me over the phone. We agreed to meet early in the morning. I couldn't wait to see what the private investigator had discovered.

Crissy was already at the park when I arrived. Her hair was swept into a ponytail like mine, and we both had on sweat suits. She hurried to give me a hug, and then she passed an envelope to me as we started to jog.

"Don't open that yet. Not until I tell you what the investigator told me. First of all, he didn't catch her in action doing anything to your car yesterday, so you may want to keep an eye on

Miss Dana. Second of all, Lesa's been seeing another man. The investigator says that it didn't appear to be a new relationship, because the two seemed real comfortable and chummy with each other. He took pictures of them going out to dinner, and of them having sex in the back of his car. The guy she's seeing is a young model who works with her. His name is Lance Bush, and he also works as a manager at some fancy store at the mall. His apartment is near yours, and he doesn't have a lot of money. Other than being nice looking, I don't know why Lesa is interested in him. I saw his dick in those pictures. Trust me when I say it's nothing to brag about."

The whole time Crissy spoke, my eyes grew wider and wider. Jonathan was going to be devastated when he found this out. Yet again, he managed to fall for a woman who was up to no good with a younger man.

"I don't know what to say. Is this guy after her money? Or should I say after Jonathan's money? Lesa doesn't have much, does she?"

"I'm not sure what you mean by much, but she makes a decent living. Jonathan has way more money than she does, but the chick isn't broke. I guess you're wondering if she could be after his money, huh?"

"Yes. When Dana was doing her little thing on the side, she was giving Jonathan's money to her lover. He was broke as hell, and he found a fool like Dana who was willing to take care of him. I just hope this isn't the case again."

"I can't answer that right now. I don't know if Lesa has a motive, but the private investigator said that she went to Jonathan's house on a few occasions and left with some clothes. He also said that she spent the night with him last night. I take it that they've possibly made up. I told the PI to keep following her."

"I'm still speechless. And I'm glad you're the one with all this evidence, not me. Are you going to tell him about her?"

Crissy stopped jogging. She placed her hands on her knees, while taking several deep breaths. "Hell, no, I'm not telling him. You are. You need to tell him what's going on with this bitch and tell him soon."

I stopped jogging too. "Absolutely not. I'm not telling him a darn thing. I was the one who broke the news to him the last time. You already know that turned out to be one big mess."

"It did, but he was very appreciative of you for telling him the truth, wasn't he?"

"If that's what you want to call it, yes, he was. And he'll be very appreciative of you for telling him what's up too. I'm not getting involved anymore. As far as I'm concerned, it's not my business."

We started to walk instead of jog. "No matter what you say," Crissy said, "Jonathan will always be your business. I'm not going to say a word to him, but I have a feeling that, eventually, you will."

I disagreed. I didn't want no part of this. We started to jog slowly again, and that's when I told Crissy about the guy I'd met at the movies.

"Don't rush into anything," she said. "Put complete closure to your situation with Jonathan. Then move on."

"I have put closure to it. He did too."

Crissy doubted me. I did a little too, but I kept my fingers crossed, hoping to leave well enough alone and stay away from chaos that would soon erupt.

CHAPTER 16

JONATHAN

A weekend vacation was what we needed. I invited Lesa to join me on a quick getaway to Vegas, and when I showed her the tickets I had already purchased, she couldn't say no.

"Jonathan, you really shouldn't have bought these," she said while standing in her tiny office, which was cluttered with colorful fabrics and papers stacked high on her desk. "I . . . I told you that I needed some space, didn't I?"

"You did, but it's been so difficult being without you. I thought we could just get away from our surroundings and figure out a way to get back to the way things used to be between us. Don't you miss that?"

Lesa sighed then placed her hand on her hip. "I do, but what good is Vegas going to do us? I don't think you understand how serious—"

"I do understand, and I can't stress enough how sorry I am. But if we want to continue this relationship, we have to be willing to put certain things behind us and start somewhere. I can't think of a better place than Vegas. There's fun, entertainment, and the weather is beautiful right now. Besides that, you will be in the presence of one sexy man who loves you dearly."

A smile washed across her face, making me feel real good. She walked around her desk to stand closer to me. "You fucked up, Jonathan, and I'm not sure if going to Vegas will change anything, but I guess it won't hurt, so when are we leaving again?"

"Soon. Like tomorrow. Get out of here, go home and pack, and I'll see you in the morning."

Lesa seemed a little hesitant, but she nodded and told me she would be ready. I was hyped about her agreeing to go with me, but when I leaned in to kiss her, she halted my actions by placing her hand against my chest.

"Not now," she said. "Don't rush me back into this."

"I'm trying not to, but I can't help myself. Besides, a little kiss won't hurt, will it?"

"A little kiss tends to lead to other things. I'm not prepared to go there just yet."

"Well, sleep on it. I intend to make your trip to Vegas so worth it, and making love to you is second on my agenda. Preparing you to become my wife is first."

Lesa smiled again, but she refused to give me a kiss. She escorted me to the door then clenched her hand together with mine.

"I don't know what the future holds for us, and I would be lying if I said I don't love you anymore. I do. That's why I'm willing to make this move with you. Don't be late picking me up, and drive safely."

The kiss I awaited had finally arrived. We indulged ourselves for several long minutes, and I pulled away when my dick started to stiffen. I immediately left, feeling like I was floating on clouds. I couldn't wait to be with her again, and, when morning came, I was thirty minutes early picking her up.

We rode to the airport and were in Vegas in no time. I opted to stay in a penthouse suite for the next three days, and the second we entered the room, our luggage hit the floor, and our bodies hit the bed. We made love for what seemed like day in and day out. It felt amazing to be inside of her without thinking of anyone else. I wasn't worried about the lies anymore, wasn't concerned about any interruptions, and I didn't concern myself about not being able to stay hard. My mind was in the right place. She seemed delighted about that too, and as I tackled her pussy in a doggie-style position, she expressed how happy she was to have me back.

"See," she said. "I knew you'd get it together. Welcome hoooome. This pussy is so glad that you're home and the doors are open again."

"Stay open. Never close, and thanks for inviting me in again."

We laughed, kissed, and continued to fuck our way throughout the entire suite. By midnight, I was exhausted. Lesa had worn me out. We sat on the balcony, chilling in a lounge chair while embracing one another. The bright lights lit up the sky, and from where we were the scenery was amazing. The warm breeze stirring was more than soothing. I felt at peace, and I could tell that she did too.

"If I could," I said, squeezing her tight, "I would marry you tomorrow."

She rubbed my chest then looked up at me with a smile. "Is that why you wanted to come here? So that we could get married?"

"Not really, but I'd be lying if I said it wasn't on my mind."

"To be honest with you, if we hadn't been through what we just went through, I would marry you in a heartbeat, but I need more time,

Jonathan. Just a little more time to make sure you're committed to me and only me."

"I am committed to you and only you, but I do understand that I have to work hard at getting your trust back. Saying it isn't going to be enough."

"It's not, but who knows? Maybe we'll come back here in a few more months and decide to tie the knot then. Or maybe we'll have the big ol' wedding that we originally talked about, and start making plans to go that route. I'll let you know what I decide. Until then, let's just enjoy the moment."

Lesa planted a soft kiss on my lips that got things heated again. She straddled my lap, and with a tight grip on her ass, I guided her up and down on my dick. Her wet pussy glazed my shaft, and it didn't take long for me to fill her with my fluids.

The weekend went off without incident. We had a fabulous time together, but on the plane ride home, I asked Lesa if she was ready to move back in with me. She said no. Her reply stunned me. I tried to understand why we couldn't work on our relationship while still living together.

"I want to give you your space," she said. "And I need mine. Just for a little while, Jonathan. If everything works out fine, then I'll move back in. Now is too soon."

"In the meantime, where are you going to live? I hate to see you living by yourself, and you do still have a lot of your belongings at my place."

"I do, and I plan on leaving them there, in hopes that I'll be coming back soon. Until then, I rented a one-bedroom apartment. I'll tell you where it is, and if you'd like to see it, just let me know. You can see it this week, when you're not too busy at work. It's not anything to brag about, and it's only temporary."

I really didn't like this, but I went with the flow. It's what I had to do, until she completely trusted me again.

Like always, work was busy. The case for Taye was underway. I spent most of my morning in the courtroom, trying to plead his case to the judge. The witnesses hadn't come forward yet, so I asked for more time. She gave me one more week. I hoped like hell that I had some solid evidence against the officers to present to her.

After court, I headed to the office. It was a little after lunch, and as soon as I got on the elevator,

I ran into Sylvia. She looked spectacular in a crisscross mustard-colored dress that showed her healthy cleavage. Her curves were nothing to play with, and her brown skin glowed. Her sweet perfume lit up the entire elevator. Her smile was like a breath of fresh air, considering what I had been through in court today.

"You . . . you look worn out," she said, holding the elevator open for me.

I yawned then held up my cup of coffee. "I am. Haven't gotten much sleep, and I've been in court all morning. Gotta go back again at three, so you already know it's going to be another long night for me."

"This is what you love, Jonathan, so stop griping. Enjoy your evening and good seeing you."

I held the door as she exited the elevator. Couldn't help it that I took a glimpse of her heart-shaped ass that jiggled underneath her dress. Looked to me as if she wasn't wearing any panties. She knew I was looking, but to wash away my thoughts, I made a sharp turn down another hallway then went into my office. Unfortunately for me, Crissy was there waiting for me.

"I need to get your signature on these papers today. You've had them on your desk since last week. I don't know what is taking you so long to sign them."

"I haven't signed them because I haven't had a chance to look them over. Tell me what they are real quick, and I might sign them."

"Can't you read?"

I placed my briefcase on my desk, along with my coffee cup. I folded my arms across my chest, shooting her a look that could kill. "I don't know what's gotten into you, but you need to get your shit together or get the hell out of my office. I don't have time for your attitude today. I won't have time for it tomorrow either or the next day after that."

"Well, how about on Wednesday or Thursday, or when you're done trying to break Sylvia's heart or the heart of every other woman you can? I need these papers signed, Jonathan. It would be nice if you would focus on the important things around here instead of your personal life."

I pointed to the door. "Out. Get out and to hell with those papers. They won't get my signature today. You'll be lucky if I sign them by Friday."

"You are such—"

"Out!" I shouted loud enough to rattle her. She stormed out of my office, calling me something underneath her breath. All I did was shake my head. I hurried to read over some notes for my next case, and within the next couple of hours, I was back in court. Stayed there until almost seven. I was beat. No words could express how happy I was to pull in my driveway and let the garage down.

Slightly on the hungry side, I stopped at the fridge to grab a leftover piece of chicken from KFC that I purchased the night before. I missed Lesa's dinners, as well as her presence. She couldn't get back here fast enough. The chicken was cold, but I heated it up in the microwave for a few minutes then grabbed a cold beer. I put the chicken into my mouth and bit down on it.

As I made my way to the bedroom, I was alarmed to see my bedroom doors closed. Then a grin appeared on my face. I had a feeling that Lesa was in there naked as a jaybird, waiting on daddy to come home. Like a kid in a candy store, I swung the door open, only to find myself several feet away from a growling pit bull that was sitting on my bed like he owned it. My smile quickly vanished. The second he showed more of his sharp teeth, I tossed the chicken bone at him and the beer can. I then jetted so fast down the hallway that I dropped my suitcase.

I slipped on the hardwood floor, and as I ran to the living room, I wasn't sure how close the pit bull was behind me. I didn't have time to turn around. I hurdled over the couch and wound up splitting the crotch area of my slacks. One of my vases crashed to the floor, and I knocked over a plant as I darted to my office. Loud barking seemed closer and closer.

The second I made it to my office, the pit bull chomped down on my ankle. I was barely able to pull my foot inside of the door before slamming it hard. He jumped on the glass doors, barking and gazing at me as if he wanted to eat me alive. My chest heaved in and out; I was completely out of breath. I felt blood trickling down my ankle, so I reached in my pocket for my cell phone. I stood with one hand against the door, trying my best to keep it closed. It wasn't an easy task, because the pit bull kept charging at the door, desperately trying to get inside. Now I wished I had gone into the kitchen where one of my guns was. It was too late to think about that, but not too late for me to tell the dispatcher I needed the cops to get here fast.

It took the police nearly ten minutes to arrive. By then, the pit bull sat calmly in front of the door, as if he hadn't planned on moving anytime soon. I was on the phone with a police officer whom I told where to find an extra key outside. He entered my house through the garage. Hearing someone come inside caused the pit bull to sit up. He started barking and growling.

The officers moved quickly. They wore protection, and as the dog charged one of the officers, the other one quickly gave the dog a shot to calm him. I felt so relieved when they got the dog under control. He was taken out of my house, and I definitely didn't want to see him again.

"You need a doctor," the officer said, looking down at my ankle. "An ambulance is on the way."

I didn't think the dog had bitten me, but he had for sure grazed me. The paramedics came, and as they took care of my ankle, I told the officers what had happened. They looked around my house for at least thirty minutes. One of the officers came into the living room where I was sitting on the couch to give me a piece of paper.

"This was on your bed," he said. "Did you read this?"

I removed the paper from his hand, opened, and read it: ALL DOGS HAVE BAD DAYS. YOU SHOULD KNOW.

"No, I didn't get a chance to read this. Like I said, the dog was on my bed. I barely made it into the room."

"Do you have any idea who could have put that dog in here?"

I shrugged. "No, I don't. This is the second incident, but I have no idea who is behind what I now consider stalking me."

I informed the officers about the note on my windshield. I also mentioned what had happened at Sylvia's place and about the scratch on her car. They said this sounded pretty serious, and asked why I hadn't reported the note.

"I wasn't sure if it was for me. At least, not until Sylvia told me what was going on with her. The dog incident confirms that someone is after both of us. I believe they've been watching us, too."

"We'll do our best to help you get to the bottom of this, but do you mind if we speak to Sylvia? She may be able to shed more light on this, and if she's reported some of the incidents, that would help during our investigation."

"Please do speak to her."

I gave the officers her contact information. They promised to be in touch. I surely hoped that they got some answers, because the person responsible needed to be dealt with ASAP.

After the police left, I called Lesa to make sure she was okay, and to tell her what had happened. She didn't answer her phone, so I left a voice mail, asking that she return my call soon. I'd thought about going over to her place, but I wanted to give her all the space she needed right now. Things had been going well between us, and I didn't want any fuckups.

While waiting for her to call back, I removed the dirty sheets from my bed and took them to the washroom to be washed. I swept up broken glass from a vase then straightened the plant I had knocked over. I also wiped smudge marks from my office doors that came from the pit bull's claws. I took a long, hot shower, and once I was done, I checked my phone to see if Lesa had called back. She hadn't. Maybe she was asleep. It was rather late. I figured she would call back if or when she got my message.

Her call never came. I tossed and turned, unable to sleep. I kept thinking about who could be responsible for this. Who had a key to enter my house and was brave enough to put a dog like that on my bed? I seriously didn't know. Neither Dana nor Lesa was at the top of my list. My mind traveled back to some of the cases I'd worked on. I even thought about that fool, Lewis McFarlin, who had been creeping with Dana. He would definitely do something like this. I made a mental note to make sure he was still behind bars. There was no question that I had enemies. But who . . . who was after me and Sylvia?

Speaking of Sylvia, I wanted to alert her that the police needed to speak to her. I called twice, but got no answer. Then, I thought, what if someone had done something tragic to her?

What if she wasn't as successful as I had been in getting away from the dog? I was starting to worry, and since I couldn't sleep, I decided to put on some clothes and go check on her. She was used to my pop-up visits. It was late, but I didn't think she'd have a problem with me stopping by.

I arrived at Sylvia's place slightly before midnight. She opened the door, looking to be wide awake, yet in shock to see me standing there.

"Wha . . . what are you doing here?" she said.

"I stopped by to make sure you were okay, and to tell you what happened at my house tonight. Nothing like what happened to you, but definitely quite scary."

Wearing a silk nightgown, Sylvia opened the door to let me inside. A sweet smell tickled my nose, and I loved the way she always kept her contemporary-decorated apartment so sleek and clean. Not everybody could do white leather couches and rugs. She did it perfectly. I guessed there was a benefit to living alone.

"Have a seat," she said. "Can I get you anything to drink?"

"No, I'd better not. But thanks, though."

I sat on the couch and began to tell Sylvia what I walked in on tonight. She seemed deeply concerned, and encouraged me to find out more about Lesa.

"Jonathan, I know you don't want to hear this, but how well do you know her? I think you're giving her too much credit. What if she's the one doing this?"

"I know her well enough to know that she's not brave enough to put a dog like that in my bedroom. That I know for sure. And I'm not giving her too much credit. She's capable of doing some things, just not that."

Sylvia scratched her head. "What I'm saying is she could have gotten someone else to do it. Besides, how did the person get into your house? No one has a key but her."

"She doesn't have a key to your place, does she? How do you think someone got in here?"

"Unfortunately, I keep an extra key underneath my mat. It was missing. It's still missing. I had the locks changed, and I also bought a gun, just in case the person who was here decides to come back. I'm not playing around with this, Jonathan. I will hurt somebody if they come in on me. I've been real uneasy around here, to the point where I kind of want to move."

"I think you have to do whatever to protect yourself, and if you feel like moving, by all means do it. I'm going to have a new alarm system put in tomorrow. One with cameras so I can catch the person in the act, if they decide to come back. I haven't been that scared in a long time. My heart was racing fast. You would have thought I was Usain Bolt, trying to get away from that damn pit bull."

Sylvia laughed then covered her mouth. "It's not funny, but as you were telling me about it, I got a picture in my head of you running away from that dog. So terrible of someone to do that, and I'm glad your injuries weren't worse."

"Shiiiit, me too. He almost got me. He was minutes away from knocking that door down and getting some of this chocolate meat."

Sylvia sat silent then picked up the remote to turn on the TV that was mounted above the fireplace. She cleared her throat. "Are you sure you don't want anything to drink?" she said. "What about some popcorn?"

"Popcorn? Why would I eat popcorn this late?"

"Because it's a good late-night snack. Besides, I was about to watch a movie before you came. Couldn't sleep and *Coming to America* is on again."

"*Coming to America?* That old movie?"

"Old, but like new every time I watch it."

Sylvia got up and went into the kitchen. She popped popcorn then returned with a bottled water and a beer. She gave me the water. "Here. Just in case your throat is dry."

I snatched the beer from her hand then gave her back the water. She sat on the couch, and we began watching *Coming to America*. We laughed at several scenes, and commended Eddie Murphy for making this one of the best films ever. Sylvia started to tell me some more of her favorite movies, and I shared some of mine.

"Oooo, I love *New Jack City*," she said. "That's another one of my favorites."

"*New Jack City* and *The Godfather*," I said. "*Scarface* is up there, too, and don't let me forget about *Primal Fear*. That movie just did something to me."

"*Primal Fear?* I don't remember much about that one, but didn't it have something to do about a lawyer or something?"

I gave Sylvia a recap. The discussion about movies turned into favorite songs. Sylvia rushed up from the couch to go get a record that she insisted I needed to hear. Before she stepped away, I reached for her hand. She turned her head and looked at me.

"Sit down," I said to her. "Just for a minute."

She inched back then slowly sat next to me.

"I just want to get a few things off my chest," I said. "First thing, I want to apologize for the way I spoke to you the other day. I know my words hurt and my tone wasn't exactly the best, but in order for you to understand why I went there, I must tell you why. The truth is Jaylin and I are good friends, but also big competitors. We always have been and always will be. When I found out about the two of you having sex, it bothered me for days. Maybe even weeks. I couldn't stop thinking about it, and he was the last person I ever thought you would do something like that with. Now, it's as if he has or has had everything I want. In no way am I jealous of him, but I just wanted something, especially a woman who I was once in love with, he couldn't have. You made it too easy, and I was upset with you. Angry to the point where I wanted to take you and shake you. I wanted you to hurt, and deep down, it is my hope that you regret being with him."

Sylvia quickly spoke up. "I do, Jonathan. I really do, but I can't change what happened between us. I know why you've been a little harsh toward me. I totally get it. I also don't believe you will ever fully forgive me. I'm not okay with us just being friends, but considering all that has happened, it's the least we can be."

She held out her hand and I shook it. "Friends," she said.

"Always," I replied. "Friends."

She walked off to get the music. We found ourselves dancing and laughing until the wee hours of the morning. By that time, I had had several drinks. So had she, and it wasn't long before she passed out on the couch and went to sleep. I planted a soft kiss on her forehead then locked the door on my way out.

side to get Jonathan's attention. My black silk blouse revealed a healthy part of my cleavage, and my black stilettos increased my height by five inches.

With my back facing the door, I glanced at the round clock on the wall, seeing that it was already ten minutes to six. I had hoped to be done by six-thirty, just so I could get home and check out my favorite show on TV. The room was kind of stuffy, and when I realized that a few beads of sweat had dotted my forehead, I reached over to the thermostat to lower the temperature. As soon as my hand touched the thermostat, I felt another set of hands on my hips. I was startled, but then again, I already knew who was behind me from the smell of his intoxicating cologne, which always left me breathless. I was shocked that he had touched me in such a way, but without saying one word, I reached my hand up to rub the back of his head.

"I need you, Sylvia," Jonathan whispered with his lips close to my ear. "I need you now."

Without hesitating, I said three words to my best friend's husband: "Take me now."

He slowly removed the buttons on my silk blouse, one by one. He then pulled it open, massaging my breasts together and manipulating my hard nipples. I squirmed from the touch of his hands, and, unable to stop this, I turned around to face him.

We stared into each other's eyes, knowing that what we were about to do was wrong on so many different levels. Jonathan, however, inched my miniskirt over the curves in my hips and eased my lace panties down to the floor. I happily stepped out of them then turned to face the copier. I bent over slightly, and displaying how flexible I was, I hiked my right leg on top of the copier, so that Jonathan could have easier access to my pussy.

He held my leg in place with one hand and unzipped his pants with the other. They dropped to his ankles, and it didn't take long for him to step out of his pants and shoes. He pressed his hardness against my butt, but that was only to tease me. I remained quiet as ever, but I held my breath when Jonathan dropped to his knees and began to take light licks between my legs. My pussy was staring him right in the face, and enjoying every bit of his delicate licks. His tongue searched deeper and hit a hot spot that caused my legs to buckle.

"Hold on, baby," he said. "I need to taste a bit more of this."

I closed my eyes and tried to focus elsewhere but couldn't. Jonathan's thick fingers kept circling my clit, and after two more minutes of his outstanding pussy-licking performance, I was ready to spray his face with my juices. He, however, stopped in mid-action and returned to standing behind me. He aimed the chunky meat on his head right at my sopping wet slit and teased the hell out of me by rubbing it against my walls. Seconds later, he inched his way in, causing me to halt my breathing again. I squeezed my eyes, thinking that my best friend's husband's dick felt even better than I ever imagined it would be. The feeling was so spectacular that I bounced my ass against him, just to bring more pleasure. The sounds of my gushing pussy juices echoed in the tiny room, and Jonathan could hear, see, and feel how excited I was to receive all that he was giving me.

"This pussy is so wet and good, baby, that I can barely stand. I want this shit to last longer, so let's move over to the chair or table," he suggested.

I hated for him to pull out of me, but when he chose to sit in the chair, I straddled him and positioned his dick to enter me again. This time,

I moved at a slow pace that caused him to drop his head back and close his eyes in thought. Jonathan held my ass and pulled my cheeks far apart so his thick meat could sink farther into me. We both moaned together, giving the chair a real workout. It squeaked, rolled around, and almost tilted over as I gave Jonathan the best ride that I could possibly give him.

It was so obvious that in this moment, and at this time, neither of us had any regrets. None, but it didn't mean that I couldn't tell that Jonathan had something heavy on his mind. The way he kept shaking his head said so, and when he lowered his head to suck my breasts, I held his face with my hands, lifting it. I sucked his thick lips with mine then stared into his serious, pain-filled eyes. I could now see the hurt in them and had started to regret my aggressiveness. A slow tear rolled down my cheek, but I continued to ride him.

"I had to do this, Jonathan," I said tearfully. "Please don't hate me for betraying Dana."

Jonathan said not one word. He rose from the chair, securing me in his strong arms. Afterward, he laid me on the floor and maneuvered his body in between my legs. I wrapped my healthy legs around him and he rubbed up and down them before entering my wetness again. He then searched into my eyes, looking for answers about his wife, who was cheating on him with a much younger man.

"I've had a rough day, Sylvia. I'm hurting and I know you have the answers for me. Please, tell me. I'm begging you to tell me if Dana is cheating on me. If so, I need to know: with who?" He dropped his head on my chest, but before he did, I could see his eyes fill with water. At that point, I wasn't sure why we were doing this. It seemed as if Jonathan was using me and trying to get answers about his wife. I knew she'd been cheating on him for a very long time, and it angered me that she could have a man as gentle and kind as Jonathan, yet not appreciate him.

So confused, I pressed my hand against Jonathan's chest for him to back away from me. His limp dick slid out of me, but I could feel a flood of my juices raining down my crack. I sat up on my elbows, looking at him and not knowing what to say.

"Jonathan, I told you before that—"

"Please!" he yelled and then slumped his head again. The loud pitch of his voice caused my eyes to widen, and he demanded to know the truth. "It is Lewis, isn't it? Just tell me, damn it! Is it Lewis?"

Refusing to answer, I quickly stood up and pulled down my skirt. Jonathan rushed up from the floor too and reached out to embrace me. This was such a horrible situation to be in, and he could see that I was about to lose it. No matter what, though, he continued to beg for answers.

"I'm begging you, Sylvia, please." He contin-ued to hold my trembling body. "Just tell me if it's Lewis. That's all I need is a yes or no."

My dry mouth finally opened. I could barely speak. Jonathan did need to know the truth. I wasn't so sure if I was willing to tell it: because I knew what Dana had done to him was wrong, or because I wanted him for myself. Either way, I whispered, "Yes," and told him that Dana had been cheating with Lewis for the past three years.

I jumped from my sleep, thinking about that day. And after tonight, a huge part of me wanted to tell Jonathan about Lesa. I remembered the backlash from telling him about Dana, but Lesa wasn't my friend. He was. He was the one who meant something to me. I just didn't know if I would be in the wrong for going there again. I didn't want him to come back to me because another woman had let him down. I wanted him to come back to me because he wanted a future with me. Because he realized he loved me, and he recognized that we belonged together. This was tough, but I knew something had to be said soon.

I searched around my apartment, but Jonathan was gone. It was almost six o'clock in the morning. Instead of going back to sleep, I went for a long, relaxing walk in Forest Park. Walking always helped to relax me, and it definitely helped to keep me in shape. I surely thought I would see Crissy on the walking trail too, but all I saw were a bunch of people walking their dogs and several people skating on rollerblades. I made a mental note to buy me some of those. They seemed to burn a lot of calories, and I was highly interested in doing whatever to keep myself in shape.

I returned to my car, tired as ever because I had run the last mile and a half back. I was happy to take a seat, so I plopped down to catch my breath. Seconds later, I started the car, but as soon as I drove off the parking lot, I heard a squeaking sound. The squeaking got louder, and when I looked down to see what it was, I saw at least ten mice moving around my feet. I could have died. I slammed the car in park and then jumped out and into the middle of the street. Another driver almost crashed into the back of my car, and he swerved to avoid me.

"Stupid idiot!" he yelled from his window then blew his horn as he sped away. I was a nervous wreck. More cars started to blow their horns, leaving me in a panic. I didn't know if I should pick up the mice one by one to get them out, or call someone to help me. Luckily for me, a man got out of his car to help. He pulled my car over to the curb, and one by one, he set the mice free. I asked him to double-check my car to make sure there were no more. He did, but I still didn't feel comfortable getting back inside of it. I did, however, see a folded piece of paper on the passenger's side seat. I reached for it then closed the door. The note read: YOU ARE A FOOL, SYLVIA. ONE, BIG, FOOL!

I put the paper in my purse, just so I could show it to the police when I went to the station to report this. Still unable to get in my car, I thanked the man for helping me then called a cab. I called a tow truck to get my car, and asked the man to take it to my mechanic. I was sure he would check it more thoroughly for me, but until then, I opted to rent a car.

This was so crazy to me, and it was the last straw. The only person I knew to go after was Dana. I was hoping that she would crack. She couldn't keep secrets for long, and if she had done this, I knew it would be a matter of time before she would explain why. I contacted her when I got home, but she stuck with her lies.

"You all are crazy! There is so much more to do in life than harass people and chase after men who are taken. I'm sick of hearing from you, Sylvia, and you must be eager to go to jail. Stop calling me or else I'm going to make your life so fucking miserable that you're going to regret ever calling yourself my friend. Good-bye!"

Dana was a good liar, but I started to feel as if she wasn't the one. I needed to follow up with Crissy to see what else the private investigator had found out. I decided against calling Jonathan to tell him what had happened, but I did go to the police department to report it. I also spoke to the officers who were at Jonathan's house last night. In my opinion, they didn't seem like they wanted to help, and were more concerned about our involvement. One claimed they needed proof. I intended to get it, only because after leaving there, I knew Jonathan and I were on our own with this. We would never hear one word from them or get any kind of follow-up. That I was sure of.

***

On Monday, Crissy wasn't in the office. She called over the weekend to tell me that she was taking a few days off to visit her cousin in Texas. I knew she needed a break, and the last thing I wanted to bug her about was the private investigator and Lesa. I hadn't confronted her yet, but since Dana was fair game, so was she. Crissy told me where Lesa worked, per the investigator's information. So around lunch, I drove to the location, only to find Lesa outside with a man who looked to be a model. They were indulged in what looked to be a heavy and intense conversation. She didn't even see me coming her way. When she spotted me, a fake smile washed across her face. I surely wondered if this was the man she had doing all of her dirt for her. He didn't look like the man I'd seen her screwing in the photo, but then again, the picture was blurred. All I knew was somebody was fucking.

"I'll see you back inside," she said to him as I approached her. "I need to speak to a friend of mine."

I hurried to correct her. "I wouldn't say we're friends at all. Please don't go there."

The man looked at both of us and hesitated before going inside of the tall brick building with numerous glass windows. Lesa folded her arms, displaying much attitude.

"Not here, Sylvia," she said. "If you want to speak to me about anything, you need to make an appointment."

I laughed. "Girl, please. You're not that important. I came to tell you a few things, so please listen up. If you don't stop what you're doing, Jonathan will soon learn about you and your little longtime lover. It seems as if you've been cheating on Jonathan for a long time, and how dare you ridicule him for being with me? I'm not going to tolerate any more of your bullshit, and just so you know, you are days away from your world tumbling down. The choice is yours. Stop or pay the price."

Lesa narrowed her eyes and winced. "I've never cheated on Jonathan before. Your accusations are false, and you are so desperate that you'll blame me for anything. You need to seek medical attention, Sylvia, and that little helpful choice, sweetheart, is yours."

"I'm not Jonathan. You can't feed me the lies. You are evil, Lesa. He will find out all about you real soon."

She threw her hand back, as if she didn't care. "Whatever. I have work to do. Go kill yourself, or please do get a life that doesn't revolve around the man I love."

She stormed away and went inside of the building. I had to laugh to myself at her for trying to be so convincing. I wished that Jonathan would see through her before it was too late.

CHAPTER 18

JONATHAN

Things were starting to fall into place again. Lesa was back on my team, Britney called to tell me how well she'd been doing in school, and Sylvia and I were considered friends again. The witnesses with the videos came forward, and the whole story made nationwide news. I was the spokesperson for my client. So many individuals were trying to get at me to discuss the next move. To say I was overwhelmed would be putting it mildly. I barely had time to handle my other cases, but somehow, I made time. There were days when I worked from six a.m. to midnight. Didn't have time for much else, but Lesa understood how important my job was to me. She had moved back in with me, and, whenever we made time for it, our lovemaking had been on point. As soon as things settled down, I intended to officially make her my wife.

My office was swarming with reporters. I did my best to get away from them, and knowing where I could go for privacy, I headed toward Crissy's office. She was on vacation, but Sylvia was sitting at her desk. I asked her to open Crissy's door, and when we went inside, I locked it.

I released a deep breath then sat on the arm of a sofa. "Have you been seeing the news?"

"Yes. This is crazy, Mr. Celebrity Lawyer. You're all over the place, and every time I turn the channel, there you are," she said. "I'm almost speechless about what those officers did. I can't say that I'm surprised. It happens all the time. They just got caught."

"Right. And what disturbs me the most is they have no remorse for attempting to ruin that young man's life. We've got to do better than this for sure."

"I agree, and I'm so proud of you for handling this case and taking it to the level that you did. You made people see Taye in a different light, and you looked sooo handsome on TV. I was like, look at him. All professional and everything. Definitely a sight for sore eyes."

I blushed. Sylvia always knew when to say the right things. Too bad she may not appreciate where this conversation was going though.

"Thank you for the kind words. I could say the same for you; you always look spectacular. On another note, how long will Crissy be out?"

"A week, maybe two. I'm not sure. She's been on edge a lot, and I've been meaning to ask you if you know what is going on with her."

I shrugged. "I've been wondering the same thing too. Honestly, I don't think she likes working here anymore. She really hasn't liked working since Mr. Duncan died, and a rich little daddy's girl is used to having things her way. That hasn't been the case since then. She doesn't like for me to call the shots, but it is what it is."

"I won't comment, because she's my friend. The two of you need to work through whatever. Try not to be so mean to her. You've been awfully mean to her, and I witnessed your tone over the phone one day."

"I was probably having a bad day. And, knowing me, I'm sure I apologized to her."

"Most of the time, you always own up to your mistakes, so I'm sure you apologized to her."

I honestly couldn't remember, but, thinking about something else, I walked over to the coffee machine. I poured a cup of coffee then sat on the sofa.

"I need to tell you something. Can you stay for a minute?" I said.

"Sure. What's up?"

I hesitated for a few seconds then let it out. "I'm planning to take Lesa to Vegas and marry her. I don't have a specific date yet, but it will be soon. Probably after all of this stuff with Taye's case simmers down."

I could see Sylvia swallow hard. She reached over and touched the top of my hand. "Good for you, Jonathan. I wish you nothing but the best, and if you believe Lesa is the woman for you, what can I do? I thank you for telling me, though. Means a lot."

"I didn't want you hearing it through the grapevine. I'm sure people around here are going to run their mouths about it, especially since many of them will be invited to a reception after we return."

"Yeah, people do talk a lot around here. But if you're sure, nothing else really matters. Are you sure this is what you want to do? Positive that you know enough about Lesa to want to marry her? I hope you are, Jonathan, because I don't want to see you get hurt again."

"I know you feel as if Lesa isn't worthy of me, but you don't know her like I do. She's a good woman, Sylvia. None of us are perfect, but deep down I know I'm making the right choice."

Sylvia slowly closed her big, round eyes then stood up. She walked toward the door, without turning to face me. "I'm sorry. I can't just sit there and pretend that this doesn't upset me when it does."

She stormed out of Crissy's office. Even though I didn't feel good about the way she felt, I still had to move forward with my plans.

When it came to romancing my woman, I was the king of it. I didn't mind going above and beyond the call of duty, and I had to throw in a little extra since I had done wrong. Lesa and I had just had dinner. I rented a private dining room where the two of us could talk, listen to jazz music, and dance. She had been wrapped in my arms all night. The more time we spent together, the more I realized she was the one for me. Besides that, her forgiveness showed me what kind of woman she was. She didn't keep throwing Sylvia up in my face like Dana had done, and she made me feel as if she was in this for a lifetime, too.

"I love you," she said as we cuddled in bed that night. "I keep thinking about the little shakeup that our relationship endured, and it seems as if it brought us closer. While I was away from you, I realized how much I didn't want to be. I'm glad you had a chance to deal with your feelings for Sylvia, and it's a good thing that you worked through them now, instead of later."

I planted a soft kiss on her forehead. "I was thinking the same thing. That's why I'm ready to do this. As soon as this case and all of this attention on it dies down, we're getting out of here. We're going back to Vegas, and you, sweetheart, are going to marry me. Scrap the big wedding. I don't need it. All I need is you. How do you feel about that?"

While naked, Lesa straddled the top of me then massaged my chest. "I can show you how I feel about it better than I can tell you. But I will say this: I'm going to enjoy being Mrs. Jonathan Tyrese Taylor."

"Not as much as I'm going to enjoy you having that status."

Lesa leaned forward to kiss me. I separated her ass checks and navigated my hard muscle inside of her warmth. The ride was slow, but as she ground hard on top of me, I picked up the pace. My strokes caused her to react wildly. She rode me with much enthusiasm, and the sounds of her pussy popping sounded off in the room.

"You're the best, baby," she shouted. "You always come through for meeeee!"

I felt the same way about her. Finally, I found a woman who was on the same page as me.

CHAPTER 19

SYLVIA

The news was tragic. My hands were tied. I couldn't do anything but use Brian to help me fuck away my pain. It wasn't as if he didn't know about my situation with Jonathan. He was well aware of it. He knew how I felt about him, and from our first conversation I told Brian that it would be difficult for me to love another. He still seemed willing to try. He considered me special, but that I was not. I used him, and he allowed me to do it. Without getting much in return, he settled for pussy that yearned to have another man inside of it instead of him. As he lay on top of me, I was like a zombie. Numb. I barely wanted to be there, and when he kissed my cheek to inquire about what was wrong, he already knew.

"Maybe we shouldn't be doing this," he said, looking down at me. "It doesn't seem as if you're with me tonight."

I wasn't there tonight or the night before. The night before that I faked an orgasm, just to get it over with. "I . . . I just don't feel good tonight. It has nothing to do with you, trust me. I ate something earlier that has my stomach feeling a little yucky."

Brian eased off of me, allowing me to go to the bathroom. I turned on the light and squinted from the bright lights above the mirror. When I looked at it, I saw my messy hair and suck marks that Brian had put all over my breasts and neck. I touched one of the suck marks on my neck then stared at the mirror, thinking about Jonathan. Tears rushed to the rim of my eyes, and, before I knew it, they started falling like rain. I grabbed my aching stomach then sat down on the toilet. While rocking back and forth, I cried harder and harder. This was tough. Losing him was harder than the last time. I wanted, needed him so badly; and as much as I tried, I just couldn't shake him. I didn't want to shake him. He needed to know what Lesa was doing behind his back, and I knew he would appreciate me for telling him the truth. There was no way in hell that I could keep this from him. No way in hell, especially since I thought it could somehow or some way benefit me.

As I cried out loudly, Brian rushed to the door. He wiggled the doorknob then knocked. "Sylvia, open the door! Are you okay?" he shouted. "Open the door. Now!"

I crawled to the door then reached for the knob. I didn't want him to see me like this, but I needed somebody, anybody to make me feel better. I fell into his arms, expecting for him to help me pick up the pieces. He held me tight, as I cried hard for another man.

"I'm sooo sorry," I hollered out and whined like a baby. *God forgive me for making such a fool of myself.* "I can't do thiiiiiis. You already know that I love someone else, but . . . but he doesn't love meee!"

"It's okay," Brian said, holding me. "Calm down. Everything will be okay."

Several minutes later, Brian carried me to my room and tucked me in bed. He put his clothes back on. I was afraid of what his thoughts were of me. I guessed he thought I was one crazy, sick bitch, and I was sure that he wanted to run, but he listened to my explanation for my behavior. I also told him about me wanting to tell Jonathan about Lesa.

"Don't tell him," he said. "You of all people should not say one word to him."

"No, I of all people should tell him. He needs to know and maybe it will change things."

"I doubt it, but I know you're going to do what you want to anyway."

"Brian, Jonathan and I have a long history together. I've known this man for a long time, and he's more than just a friend. If you knew something like this about one of your friends' future wife or husband, wouldn't you want them to know?"

"It depends. But considering that this is how it all went down the last time, with him and his first wife, I don't know if you would want to be that person to interfere again."

"Okay, I'll make this easier for you. If you were about to marry a woman who was cheating on you, wouldn't you want to know? No matter who delivers the message, wouldn't you still want to know?"

He was silent for a moment then nodded. "I guess I would. But pray on this and make sure it's the right thing to do."

I was thankful to Brian for our discussion. And while he didn't stay the night with me, by morning my mind was made up. I was going to tell Jonathan what the private investigator had passed on to Crissy. I was sure there was more, so I waited until more information could be shared.

***

Sure enough, when Crissy came back to the office, she filled my ears with more things about Lesa. The private investigator had been following her for weeks. During her separation from Jonathan, she lived with her lover. She still visited him, mainly during the morning hours, and she had also been kicking up a new relationship with another model who lived in New York. According to the investigator, they hooked up after one of her fashion shows, went to dinner, then had sex the same night. Crissy also shocked me when she told me he saw her visit an abortion clinic. Days later, she returned to have the procedure done. This was enough for me to change Jonathan's mind about making her his wife. I was eager to share the news.

The following day, I put my game face on and headed to his office. I wanted to see if he could schedule a day and time to talk to me, but when I got there, his secretary informed me that he had left for Vegas last night.

"Last night," I said in a high-pitched tone. "What time?"

"Around nine o'clock. He won't be returning for a few days. He asked that I take all messages. Would you like to leave a message for him?"

My heart sank to my stomach. What if he was already married? What if I was too late?

Damn. Damn. Damn. I rushed to my desk but halted my steps when I saw Crissy standing by the boardroom, waiting to go inside. She was talking to another staff member. I hated to interrupt her.

"Do you have a minute?" I asked.

"Sure," she said then followed me into the hallway and into the staircase. "What's going on, Sylvia?"

"Jonathan. Jonathan left to go get married. I have to stop him, Crissy. I can't let this happen. I need to go. I need to get on a plane as soon as possible and go. Help me, and please tell me that I'm doing the right thing."

"Look, you know how I feel about Jonathan, but do what's in your heart. If you want to go, then go. Just let me know and I'll call the airport to make arrangements for you."

"Would you really do that for me? I know this must seem crazy, but you know how much I love him. I can't let him make the same mistake again."

"I've never been in love before, so I wouldn't understand. Stop trying to explain this to me, and get out of here. I'll send you a text with the boarding information. Be sure to contact me when you get to Vegas, and I'll see if I can get detailed information regarding his whereabouts from his secretary."

"Please do. I have no idea what hotel he's at or anything."

"I'll find out." Crissy gave me a hug. "Be careful and go. Go now."

I rushed out of the office building then made my way to my car. Within the hour, Crissy had hooked up everything for me. She sent me a text message, letting me know where Jonathan was. I even had the room number. I boarded the plane in fear of what would happen in Vegas, but wishing that Jonathan would see the light and finally dump Lesa.

The entire plane ride, I couldn't stop thinking about all that we'd been through. I was sure his heart would be broken, but just like the last time, I intended to be there and help him get through this. I reflected back to when my husband was killed many years ago. Jonathan was the one who had been there for me. Dana was considered my best friend, but technically it was Jonathan who had my back. He encouraged me to live on. Offered me a job, just so I could have enough money to pick up the pieces. My husband didn't have insurance, so Jonathan was the one who had paid for his funeral expenses. He gave me money to settle our overwhelming bills, and he purchased a new vehicle for me after our car had been wrecked in the fatal accident my husband had. My history with Jonathan was deep. I had so many reasons to love this man, and no matter how hard I tried, I just couldn't give up on us.

I arrived in Vegas a few hours later. Not knowing if Jonathan was already a married man, I hurried off the plane, flagged down a cab, and asked him to rush me to the hotel where Jonathan was. It was already almost three o'clock in the afternoon. I prayed that I wasn't too late. With him being in a private suite, I was delayed even more. I had to persuade one of the bellhops to take me to the floor where Jonathan was. After I offered him one hundred dollars, he was more than willing.

"Down the hall and straight ahead," he said. "And please don't tell anyone I did this for you. I could lose my job."

I thanked the man, telling him I wouldn't say a word. Nervous as hell, I walked to the door with my legs trembling. I wasn't looking my best, but I didn't have time to change clothes from earlier. The plain linen dress I wore had numerous wrinkles. My hair needed to be brushed, and my makeup had all sweated off. In addition to that, my peep-toe heels were hurting my feet.

I tapped lightly on the door, but when no one answered, I knocked harder. There was a DO NOT DISTURB notice on the door, but I didn't travel this far to abide by it. I could hear someone on the inside coming toward the door.

"Room service," I said. "May I come in?"

The door swung open. My heart dropped again.

"I didn't . . ." Jonathan paused when he saw me standing there. He was dressed in a burgundy cotton robe, and house shoes covered his feet. His forehead was lined with thick wrinkles, and much anger washed across his face. "What are you doing here?" he said. "Sylvia, please don't do this. Not now."

"I'm sorry, but I have to, Jonathan. Is Lesa in there? We all need to talk, and I want her to confess to something."

I seemed to have Jonathan's attention. He widened the door, allowing me to enter the immaculate suite that was designed for the rich and/or famous. There were beautiful chandeliers hanging, a baby grand piano in the far corner, a wet bar in another, and a sunken living room area that displayed a circular, white leather couch. Many windows surrounded the suite, and the view of Las Vegas was breathtaking.

"What exactly is she supposed to confess to?" he questioned.

"Is she here? I'll let her tell you."

"No, she's not here. She's at a spa. Now, tell me what in the hell is going on right now. Does this have something to do with the stalker?"

I swallowed the huge lump in my throat and began to spill my guts. "No, but Lesa has been lying to you. She's involved with another man. They've been together for a long time, and she recently started seeing someone else who lives in New York. Also, she had an abortion a few weeks ago. I believe it was right before she moved back in with you. She's not being real with you, Jonathan. I couldn't let you go through with this, without knowing the truth."

Jonathan stared at me with a hard gaze. He was so still that I couldn't even tell if he was breathing. His brows were arched inward and his right hand had tightened into a fist.

"Don't you dare come in here and lie to me like this!" he shouted. "Oh, my God, Sylvia, why would you do this? It's over, baby. I'm so sorry, but it is over! You've got to accept this."

"No!" I shouted back. "I don't care if it's over! I'm telling you the truth. I wouldn't come this far to lie to you, and you know I wouldn't!"

"Where's your proof? I need evidence. Show me something or get the hell out of here!"

Unfortunately, I didn't bring anything with me. I had rushed out of the office and forgot to ask Crissy for pictures, notes, anything the private investigator had given her. "I don't have proof. All I have is my word."

He broke it down to me loud and clear: "Your word don't mean shit."

My heart dropped to my stomach. His words stung. Stung so bad that I felt as if my heart had been ripped from my chest. "Jonathan, please don't say that. You have to believe me. You know me, and you know I wouldn't lie about anything like this. If you don't believe me, call Crissy. Ask her. She'll tell you. She's the one who hired the private investigator to check things out."

He wasn't buying what I was selling, so I reached in my pocket for my cell phone. Thankfully, Crissy answered. I calmed down to speak to her. "Please tell him about what the private investigator told you. He doesn't believe me, and I need for him to believe that I didn't come all this way to lie."

Crissy told me to give Jonathan the phone. He snatched it from my hand and listened to her tell him what she'd told me. He didn't budge. Didn't say one word, just hit the END button then tossed the phone like he was a pitcher, throwing a baseball. It smashed into a lamp, causing it to hit the floor and break.

"Damn!" he said with tightened fists. "I'll be fucking damned!"

My heart raced. I witnessed how upset he was. Been here, done this before. I wasn't sure if I should speak up or allow him to say what was on his mind.

"I can't believe this shit! Why in the hell do I keep—"

He paused when the door came open. In walked Lesa, looking all dolled up in a bright yellow dress, a big straw hat and strappy heels that made her taller. Her smile quickly vanished as she saw me standing there. She observed the evil look on Jonathan's face.

"Answer this," Jonathan shouted with his finger pointed at her. "Are you seeing someone else, and did you have a got-damn abortion?"

Her mouth opened wide. She stepped farther into the room, shaking her head from side to side. "No!" she replied then looked at me. "Are you kidding me? Is that why you're here? Did you tell him those lies?"

"Do not talk to her," Jonathan barked. "I asked you a question. I need some answers right now!"

She turned her attention to Jonathan. "I already answered your question. I said no. I'm not seeing anyone else, and I haven't had an abortion. I can't believe that you're standing there asking me this. This is bullshit, Jonathan, and you know it!"

Lesa was good. She stood her ground, even when Jonathan threatened to call Crissy and the private investigator who had been watching her.

"You do whatever you have to do!" she shouted. "And if this so-called private investigator has something on me, show it to me. The only thing that he may be able to present is exactly what I told you already. I almost gave in to somebody who was interested in me. We . . . He performed oral sex on me and that was it. The only reason I gave him permission to do that was because you were screwing this bitch!"

"You didn't tell me that he performed oral sex on you, so get your lies straight! I'm glad it's all coming out now, and who in the hell's baby were you carrying?"

Lesa stepped closer to Jonathan with gritted teeth. I wanted him to punch that bitch in her face for lying, but I suspected that he wouldn't put his hands on her. I stayed back, nervously watching this all play out.

"I just told you that I wasn't pregnant! But if I was, I would surely get rid of the baby. I damn sure wouldn't want to be pregnant by a damn fool like you, and any nigga who believes everything his ex tells him is an idiot!

She can have your limp-dick ass. I'm so glad that I didn't marry you! Sooo glad, and you will never have to worry about me again!"

Lesa reached up and slapped the hell out of Jonathan. The smack was so loud and hard that I thought she had slapped me. I wanted him to lay her ass out, but he wasn't that kind of man. He reached for her arm and shook her real hard.

"Don't put your hands—"

He was interrupted by the spit she released in his face. He shoved her backward, causing her to stumble. She hopped on one foot to keep her balance then she removed her heel. The real Lesa showed up, and I was glad that he got an opportunity to see who she really was. As she charged at him with the shoe, he pushed her backward again. This time, she skidded across the marble floor, landing right at my feet.

"If you touch me one more time, you will be arrested," he said. "Now, get the fuck out of here, and chalk up your losses."

"My losses." She laughed then peeled herself off the floor. "Nigga, please. You're the one who lost out. You just don't know it yet."

She gawked at me, as if she was coming for me next.

"Think before you act," I said. "I am not Jonathan and I will do exactly to you what you're contemplating doing to me."

Lesa mean mugged me then removed her other shoe. She threw it at Jonathan, but he ducked to avoid it. As he charged our way, she rushed to the door. She knew that spitting on him was the last straw and she was about to catch hell. Before leaving, though, she paused to share a few words with me.

"Bitch, I'll see you around. This is not by any means over with."

The door slammed, causing me to sigh a little from relief. It was good to know that Jonathan hadn't already married her, but I wasn't sure about his current state of mind.

"Well, I guess we now know who was responsible for everything that happened. I bet she had someone she knows do that crap, probably her lover," I said.

Jonathan walked to the door and opened it. "I need some time alone, Sylvia. Give me some time."

"Sure," I said, walking to the door. "I'm staying at the Venetian, if you want to talk later. And I'm not leaving until tomorrow night."

He didn't respond. I walked out, anticipating that everything would be okay.

and I wanted to choke the life out of her. Maybe not as much as I wanted to hurt him for his betrayal. How dare he treat me that way? How dare he disrespect me in front of her? Why in the hell would he believe her over me? Whether I had been having sex with anyone, he would never know. It wasn't relevant, because what had occurred between me and Lance only happened because of what I witnessed between Jonathan and Sylvia.

I was willing to forgive him for several specific reasons. First, I had to admit that, prior to this setback with Sylvia, Jonathan was the best. He treated me well. Put me in a comfortable situation where I was more than happy to accept his proposal and eventually become his wife. Two, sex between us had been off the chain. He had mad skills in the bedroom, and every woman wanted a man who knew how to please her. It was almost as if he had gone to school to know every part of a woman's body and perfect how to please her. I'd had no complaints until recently. Third, he was loaded with money. Only the people close to him knew his net worth. It was nothing to sneeze about. He was definitely in a position to offer me a lifetime of stability and security. I was certainly looking forward to it, and having access to his money was a plus.

With or without his money, I was on the right path with my fashion design career. I still wasn't where I wanted to be financially, but that didn't matter to Jonathan. As long as I had a promising career, that's all he cared about. I'd moved in with him to save money. My previous apartment cost almost two grand a month. It felt good to bank that money, especially now when I needed it the most. It also felt good that during our time together Jonathan had been giving me money, too. I didn't want for much, and I was able to buy pretty much anything I wanted. He never questioned how much money I spent on things, nor did he complain about what I'd bought. I had much freedom in our relationship. It was almost like a dream come true for me. That all changed now that Sylvia was permanently back in the picture. I hated her, and I hated him, too.

I paced the floor in my apartment, thinking of a million and one ways to break Sylvia's neck. She crushed my big dreams in a major way. I wanted to slice that heifer's throat while in that hotel room; and the smirk on her face as Jonathan and I argued made me cringe.

I guessed that the two of them were now back together. He probably escorted her to one of those little chapels in Vegas to exchange *I do's*.

The thought of it made me sick to my stomach, but there wasn't much that I could do about it at this point. I had shown my ass. Spit on the man and called him a nigga. He would never forgive me for that, but I didn't care. I hated to be accused of things by someone who was just as guilty as I was. Jonathan had no right to treat me that way, and one day, he would regret losing me.

I didn't like to be so ugly, but the more I thought about it, maybe things had turned out for the best. If I had married Jonathan and all of this came about, it wouldn't have been pretty. Grits wouldn't have been the only thing I was cooking—maybe something with poison in it. I was seconds away from tossing those grits on his ass that night, but then I decided against it, only because I honestly wanted things to work. But marrying him would have put me in a different place. As his wife, I wouldn't have tolerated his mess. I very well would have plotted his demise and buried him with no regrets. After that, I would have happily cashed in on his money as a grieving widow and lived happily ever after, probably with another man who was willing to do right by me. But things didn't get that far. He was lucky. *She* was lucky. The way I saw it, I was lucky too.

I turned around, looking at my backup plan as he lay naked in bed, resting peacefully. I hadn't intended on being with Lance, but when things didn't go according to plan, I had to make moves elsewhere. Lance had been in love with me for quite some time. I wasn't feeling him at first, but I was grateful to him for helping me pick up the pieces after my heartbreak.

Lance slowly cracked his eyes open, only to see me standing there looking at him. He smiled then patted the spot in front of him on the bed. "What are you doing up so early?" he asked. "You need to get back in this bed and finish what you started, Miss Lady."

I didn't mind finishing what I started. I was okay with running away from what wasn't good for me as well. That would be Jonathan Tyrese Taylor. As far as I was concerned, he and that bitch he was with could burn in hell. I was done with them both.

CHAPTER 21

JONATHAN

I lay in bed, disappointed and devastated like hell. Didn't know how I'd gotten myself in a situation like this again. Why couldn't I keep a woman happy? Why did they always have to cheat? Why pretend that you wanted to be with somebody when you were in the arms of another? I just didn't get it, but then again, yes, I did. I hadn't been on the up-and-up either, but even if I had been, it appeared that, prior to my relationship with Sylvia, Lesa had already been seeing someone else. I brought her into my home because I thought she was the one. I truly thought I had someone special, and, aside from my setback with Sylvia, I was ready to be all that Lesa needed me to be. I was so hyped about Vegas, and it was unfortunate that it wound up turning into a disaster.

Thing was, I couldn't say that I hadn't been warned. I hated that Jaylin was right. Why couldn't I see the things in Lesa as he had? Why did I ignore the signs? This wasn't the first time I ignored them, and that made me feel more foolish.

And then the baby. Dana lost our baby, and now this. There was always a child involved. I couldn't help but to think about if Lesa's baby was mine. Hell, what if it wasn't? Would she lie to me and say that it was? Make me raise another man's baby, knowing damn well that I wasn't the father? I had so many questions, but I didn't want to know the answers. The answers wouldn't do me any good, because it was over. No woman would ever spit on me, refer to me as a nigga, and then see me in her presence again.

The truth was I should've taken more time to get to know more about her. Two years wasn't enough. Hell, five years wasn't in some cases, and this was on me. I swept too many things under the rug. I rarely questioned her late nights, didn't inquire about her phone calls in the middle of the night, nor did I get to know the people she referred to as her friends. Had I dug a little deeper, I would've discovered more about her. I was shocked by the way she'd clowned on me.

And then to call Sylvia ghetto; she had no room to talk. I didn't care how upset she was, but the slap, the shoe throwing, and the name calling was uncalled for. I didn't want that kind of woman in my future. Hell no. I could do without it. She was the one who had fucked up and attempted to use Sylvia like the shit was justified.

Well, Sylvia didn't make her seek not one but two lovers. She didn't make her have an abortion, and she didn't make her put up with a limp dick, so she said. She was trying to get me where it hurt. I admit that she did, but, just like the last time, I had to find a way to pick up the pieces and carry on.

Later that day, I checked out of the hotel and took the first flight back home. It was extremely embarrassing for me to contact some of the people close to me and tell them the reception had been cancelled. Basically, there would be no wedding because the woman I was supposed to marry wasn't really who she claimed to be.

"Wow, I'm sorry to hear that, Daddy," Britney said. "I'm speechless right now, and I can't believe Sylvia came all that way to tell you the truth."

Britney had always wanted Sylvia and me to be together. She was crushed when we parted ways, but the last thing on my mind right now was Sylvia.

"That was nice of her to do," I said. "I'll be sure to thank her. Meanwhile, how have you been doing? We've been playing phone tag a lot. I feel as if you've been hiding from me. When are you coming home to visit?"

"Soon. I'm just trying to get familiar with all of this stuff about the law. How did you do this? These classes are hard. It takes a brilliant person to get through this. I don't know if I'm cut out for it."

"Yes, you are. Don't talk about what you can't do, and focus on what you can do. All you have to be is determined. And you know I'm here for you. If you have any questions on your assignments, just let me know."

"Ooookay. Keep your head up too. I wish I was there to give you a big ol' hug, but since I'm not, why don't you try calling Sylvia? She's nice and—"

"I don't feel like being bothered. I would like a hug from you, though, and if you don't get here within the next few months, I'm coming to see you."

"I told you I'm coming. I got a surprise for you, too, and trust me when I say you're going to love it. Then again, I'on know."

"Yeah, that's what I'm afraid of. Good-bye, Britney. I love you."

She laughed. "Love you too."

Talking to my daughter always made me feel better. Working did, too, so I did what I knew best and dove right in. I thought about calling Jaylin to tell him how things had turned out, but I was in no mood to hear him talk about how right he was. Instead, I called the planner who assisted me with the arrangements for the reception. I asked her to contact some of the individuals I invited and let them know it was cancelled. I didn't feel like answering questions; I knew there would be plenty.

At one in the morning, I was in my home office getting some work done. There was still a lot of buzz around Taye's case that had been dropped. Several people had been reaching out for me to help them too, and, unfortunately, there was already another case in the news about three police officers filing a false claim about a crime the black man insisted he didn't commit. I was watching the news when I received an unexpected phone call from Crissy. I had been meaning to call her, but she beat me to it.

"I know it's late, but I wanted to check on you," she said.

"I didn't think you cared, but I'm doing fine."

"Jonathan, you know I care. It's just that we don't always click when it comes to business. As far as I know, you're going to be my business partner for a long time. I care about your well-being, and don't you ever forget that."

"I was feeling better, until you said that we'd be business partners for a long time," I said jokingly. "I was hoping that you would be done with the business and go do something that you really enjoy doing."

"Oh, I love what I do. Wouldn't have it any other way. Like father, like daughter; you know what I mean."

I couldn't help but to think about me and Britney. Maybe she would work at my firm one day, too. I was looking forward to it. "Yeah, like father and daughter. I'm sure your father is proud of you for doing all that you do."

"I'm sure he is too. But other than that, how are things with you and Lesa? Have you spoken to her since you've been back from Vegas?"

"Nope. We really don't have much to say to each other, and we pretty much finalized everything in the hotel room. I'm surprised Sylvia didn't tell you about it."

"I haven't spoken to her. She called and said that she was staying in Vegas until the weekend, just to get her head straight. She's really been through a lot with you. I can't help but to ask if you see a woman like her in your future."

"Truthfully, I'm not even thinking about me and Sylvia at this moment. Why is everyone trying to push us together? I'm not feeling us the way I used to, and I prefer that we remain friends."

"Well, friends do have sex and friends do lean on each other when in need. I know that all too well. Been there and done that before."

"If you say so. I need to get back to what I was doing, but before we go, send that package to me that the private investigator showed you. I want to see all of it. While it doesn't make one bit of a difference, I just want something to throw in Lesa's face if she ever comes here talking shit. I know she's coming to get her things. I just don't know when. This time, her shit will be packed."

"Good for you. I'll gather everything and send it to you in the morning."

Unfortunately, by morning I hadn't gotten any sleep. I was still in my office, working on an upcoming case. My phone rang again. This time, it was Jaylin. I hesitated to answer, but then I figured that he would find out sooner rather than later that he was right.

"It's too early," I said, answering my phone. "Don't you ever sleep?"

"Big dreamers and thinkers don't sleep. They're always cooking up something, so I called to see if you would like to invest in another big property venture I'm seeking to get my hands on in Detroit. The area is booming right now. Millionaires can easily be made."

Jaylin provided more specifics about the deal. I told him to count me in. We also talked about how Taye's case panned out. He teased me about becoming an up-and-coming star.

"I saw you on TV. You think you bad, don't you?" he said then laughed.

"I know I'm bad. Badder that your attorney Frick is, but you'll never admit it."

"Pull back, bro. You ain't that bad yet, but I gotta give credit where it's due."

"So do I. And what I mean by that is you're good. Good at knowing things about women that I don't know. Lesa and I are done. She was cheating with two other men, and she had an abortion that I didn't know about."

I continued to tell Jaylin about what had happened in Vegas. When I told him she called me the "N" word and spit on me, he interrupted.

"Yeah, that's a wrap. No woman should go there, and you should have smacked her ass into the next day. I'm glad you came to your senses.

You may want to thank the hell out of Sylvia for stopping you from making a big, huge mistake. Have you spoken to her?"

"Naw, not since I've been home. I got so much on my mind right now. I can tell you that this shit don't feel good."

"No, it doesn't. Women act like they're the only ones who go through shit. We do too, and I understand your pain. But the cure to that pain is money. Fall in love with it, and you'll always have yourself a real winner."

"I'm already in love with it. Let me know when you need me in Detroit. I'll be there."

We concluded our conversation, and I got back to what I had been working on. I quickly thought about how I hadn't thanked Sylvia for preventing me from making one of the biggest mistakes of my life. I figured she was upset with me for leaving Vegas so abruptly, but I intended to go see her real soon.

CHAPTER 22

SYLVIA

Jonathan got the hell out of Vegas. I didn't even get a chance to say good-bye. While I figured he would be upset, I wondered if he was upset with me. He hadn't contacted me to say one word. I felt some kind of way about it, too, especially since I had come all this way hoping for a better outcome between us. I wasn't going to be the one to call him first, and the least he could do was call to thank me.

Instead of going home, I stayed a few more nights in Vegas. I spoke to Brian while I was there, and his conversation helped to put me at ease. He wasn't sure if I had done the right thing. He also seemed concerned about Jonathan not reaching out to me.

"The least he could do is thank you for traveling that far to save him. I don't know what kind of man wouldn't at least do that."

"I agree, but you know what, Brian? Let's talk about something else. You've been so patient with me, and I know you get tired of always hearing about me and my ex. You mentioned that you were looking for another job. Any luck?"

"I think so. I had an interview at GMAC. They're hiring for the third shift. I would love to work there. Say a prayer for me, and I'll say one for you too."

Brian was really a nice guy. Most men were in the beginning, and there was so much more about him that I didn't know. Thing was, I wasn't so sure about dating him. We just didn't click like I needed us to. He was more of a companion to me than he was anything else.

We talked for a little while longer, and then I headed to the casino to play blackjack. I was up $700, so I called it quits and returned to my room. I knocked out eight hours of sleep, and the next day I headed back to St. Louis.

The second I got home, I unpacked my bags, and after I took out the trash that had been left there for days, I also cleaned my kitchen. I was ready for another nap, but as soon as I got comfortable in bed, there was a knock at the door. I tightened my robe then went to the door to see who it was. On the other side stood Jonathan. His head was down, but I could see his flowing waves.

I opened the door, and he was staring face to face with me.

"I came to thank you for always being there for me," he said. "May I come in?"

No, was what I wanted to say. I was bitter about how things had turned out in Vegas, but I didn't want my griping to turn him away. I knew he'd been going through hell too, so I decided to widen the door and let him come inside. Jonathan strutted in, casually dressed in jeans and a button-down silk shirt that fit his frame as if it was tailored. One by one, he undid the buttons while keeping his eyes locked on me. I opened my mouth to tell him to leave, but he immediately kept me silenced when he covered my mouth with his. The sound of our wet lips smacking sounded off in the room. It wasn't long before we started stripping off each other's clothes. A pile of our clothes were stacked behind me as I stood naked. Jonathan reached for my waist, pulling my warm body to his.

"Thank you, again, for saving my ass," he said. "I owe you."

"Yes, you do, and thank you for spreading my ass."

That's exactly what he did, when he moved me over to the couch and bent me over. His dick filled me to capacity and my pussy juices ran over. My breasts wobbled as he pushed me forward with rhythmic thrusts. The feel of him was so spectacular that I could barely stand. My legs shuddered, and with his fingers tickling my clit, I couldn't take it. I jerked forward, causing his meat to quickly exit my precious hole. He held his heavy meat, while I positioned myself on my back. He kneeled in front of me then placed my legs against his chest. With my ass barely situated on the couch, he entered me again. His eyes slowly shut; so did mine. All I felt was his long inches working me over. His hands massaged my breasts, and his tongue tantalized my nipples. I was being completely worked over and loved every minute of it. Loved it so much that I removed my legs from his chest to spread them wide like a V. He instructed his mushroom head to toy with my clit, and after his dick traveled from my mouth, back to my pussy, I came all over him. He quickly buried his face between my legs, sucking me up like a brand new vacuum cleaner. My pussy remained hot to the touch, and from the floor to the door, we explored sex in more ways than one. I wasn't sure if Jonathan still had it in him, but he left me wishing that we could go on like this forever.

***

The next day, nothing needed to be said or done. Jonathan strutted around the office as if he was a new man. I certainly felt like a new woman. I didn't want anything or anyone to ruin my day, but there was always something to deter me from my good mood. I got a phone call from Dana, telling me that it was urgent for us to speak. She left the message on my voice mail, but I deleted it. I was so done with her. At this point, I didn't care what she had to say. The devil was trying to steal my joy, but not today.

After work, I headed to Applebee's to meet Brian for dinner. He had been so nice to me; I didn't want to cancel. He was all smiles when I got there. I found out why after we sat at a booth and ordered drinks.

"I got the job," he said with a wide smile. "I start next Monday, provided that everything checks out with my drug test. I know it will, unless weed is still in my system from high school."

We both laughed. I congratulated him on getting the job. "I'm happy for you, and I know how much you wanted this. I prayed that everything worked out, and isn't God good?"

"Very good. We prayed that my situation worked out, but how about yours? Is everything working out for you, too?"

"I don't want to get ahead of myself, but things are good. I'm seeing some progress with some of the things I want, but I'll have to wait and see."

"I take it the progress you're speaking about is with you and Jonathan, right?"

"Mmmm, maybe. Like I said, I don't want to get ahead of myself. His relationship with Lesa is completely over, but I'm not exactly sure where that leaves us. I'm giving him time to take in all that happened. Eventually, we'll get around to talking about us."

Brian picked up a chip then dipped it in salsa. He put it in his mouth and chewed. "If you don't mind me asking, did he thank you yet?"

I thought about last night. Hell, yeah, he thanked me, and then some. "Yes, he thanked me. As a matter of fact, he couldn't stop thanking me."

"I guess that means the two of you had sex then. He thanked you by offering you sex."

This conversation was starting to make me feel uncomfortable. "I really don't want to say, Brian. Can we talk about something else?"

"Of course we can, but can I be honest with you about a few things?"

"You can always be honest with me. Say whatever it is that you need to say."

"From a man's perspective, I believe that Jonathan is using you. When a man is hurt, he turns to women who are willing to comfort him. You told me yourself that he did it before. Why wouldn't he do it again? You're going to get hurt, Sylvia. I really wish that you would give us a chance, instead of going back to a man who will not show you anything different."

I swallowed the lump in my throat. I hated for anyone to try to tell me about Jonathan. I knew him well, and for anyone to say that he was using me, it was a far stretch. Yes, I had thought so before myself, but only when I was mad and was looking for a reason to talk myself out of loving him.

"I appreciate you for offering things from your perspective, but I have to disagree with you about Jonathan using me. We have this thing that not too many people can understand. He knows that I have his best interest at heart. He knows that I will be there for him, and he knows that I love him with every fiber of my being. I have his back, and isn't that what a man wants? Isn't that what he needs?"

"It is, but there are many men who take advantage of those things. I'm not sitting here like I'm all that, and to be truthful, I don't have Jonathan's money. I can't afford to have a stay-at-home wife, and the woman in my future may have to get out and work. I can't go to the mall and shop for the finest clothes. These jeans I have on are about six or seven years old, but they're clean. My woman will be clean, too, but I don't have Saks Fifth Avenue money to give her."

"Sooo, where are you going with this? Jonathan is unique in his own little way, and I'm not expecting every man I meet to be like him."

"You'll soon get where I'm going, and the bottom line is this: I'm offering you me, as I am. I've treated you kind, I've respected you, prayed for you, and even advised you on certain things that didn't necessarily benefit me. My house is small; I have two dogs and a daughter who just went to trade school. Are you willing to give us a chance? If not, I'd like to consider this our final dinner."

I liked Brian, truly I did, but I wasn't at a point where I wanted a relationship with him. Why wasn't it okay for us to just be friends, and what was the rush?

"I feel as if you're giving me an ultimatum. I've barely known you for two months, and you want me to commit. And if I don't, it's good-bye? That's kind of harsh, isn't it, Brian?"

"Hold up a minute. I didn't say commit. I said give us a chance. Open up, and let's focus on me and you, instead of you and Jonathan. I get that you're in love with him, but allow yourself to fall in love with someone else. Especially since, deep down, you know he hasn't been one hundred with you. You know something isn't right, but you keep telling yourself that everything is all good. That he'll come around and things will get better. You let him call all the shots, and you're the one in fear of losing him. He should be the one in fear of losing you, but he's not, because you've made it too easy for him. I've been on these reckless paths before. I got off that path, and I don't mind getting off again. If you don't want to proceed with me, no hard feelings."

I had to see what this thing with Jonathan would lead to, especially with Lesa now being out of the picture. It was a risk that I was willing to take. If Brian couldn't understand that, oh well. "Your timing is off, Brian. I'm sorry, but it is so off right now. I can't find the time or energy to open the door for another man. That's—"

"Shhh," he said, reaching across the table to touch my hand. "Let's finish dinner and call it a night. And for the record, my timing isn't off. It's yours."

He left me with that. I gave him a hug after dinner and stood by my decision not to involve myself with another man.

CHAPTER 23

JONATHAN

Detroit was the real getaway I needed. I was having a good time with Jaylin and his best friend, Shane. We had been in meetings for the past two days. They were productive and worthy meetings that could impact our lives in a major way. I finally got an opportunity to see, up close and personal, businessmen make multimillion-dollar deals. It was a good feeling, and I was proud to be on board.

My life back in St. Louis was still a little rocky though. Lesa stopped by to finally get the rest of her belongings. We didn't say one word to each other. I actually left the house before she did. Went to the grocery store, just to get out of the way. When I returned home, my key was on the table, along with a note that said: GOOD RIDDANCE, BASTARD. It appeared to be the same handwriting as some of the notes I'd been given before, so I now knew who had been doing slick shit behind my back. She was, indeed, crazy. It didn't make me feel good that I kept finding myself with those kinds of women, but for now I planned to take it easy. While I knew that Sylvia wanted more from me, I was in a position where I wasn't going to spend much time on serious relationships.

It was time to celebrate. The meetings were done, and I was hyped. Jaylin invited me to a private party in Bloomfield Hills. By nine o'clock we were ready to go. We arrived fifteen minutes later, and for the third time that day, I was in awe. Normally, I didn't get off into lavish cars, houses, boats; all that material shit that didn't really matter, but I would be lying if I said it didn't feel good to see with my own eyes. The house we entered was almost indescribable. It hosted people from wall to wall. The contemporary décor was so unique, and there were many glass staircases, waterfalls, statues, televisions, swimming pools; it was out of this world. Made me feel like my house in St. Louis was Section 8 property. Nonetheless, I was proud of the home I had built my first year as a lawyer. I had done plenty of updates since then, but after seeing this, it encouraged me to do some more updates.

While Shane was on his cell phone, Jaylin introduced me to the owner and one of his business partners, Mr. Chan. He was real laid back, and funny as hell.

"John-John," Mr. Chan said, looking around at the crowds of people in his house. "Have whatever you want. That goes for the pretty girls around here, too, and the food isn't bad at all. Chinese cuisine is the best thing for your body. The Peking roasted duck is muuuah."

"Sounds good," I said, "but lead me to the special fried rice, extra eggs, no onion. I'm good with that for sure."

We laughed. He attempted to give us a quick tour around his place, but that wasn't successful, because either he was being stopped for conversation or Jaylin stopped to holler at someone. I wasn't sure where Shane had gone, until I looked high up on one of the staircases and saw him speaking to an attractive young woman in a sexy outfit that revealed her shapely curves. I wondered how in the hell Shane was concentrating on the conversation; it would be difficult for me to do. She reached out to touch his dreads then I saw him lean in closer to her ear. I couldn't help but to think about his wife, Tiffanie, who obviously wasn't here.

Jaylin nudged my arm to get my attention. "Let's hit up the pool area. Some food is out there, too, and I want to introduce you to some more people."

I followed him, checking out the smiles on so many women's faces and enjoying the company I was in. Everybody kept telling me that they knew me from TV. They had plenty to say about Taye's case, and it took nearly forty-five minutes to get outside, because I kept conversing with people and so did Jaylin. One female in particular wasn't letting him breathe. She kept whispering in his ear and saying something that made him blush. She was bad, too, and with a short, layered haircut and sexy-ass brown eyes, she reminded me of his wife. I wondered if he'd thought the same thing too. I sensed that they knew each other. Well. The soft kiss he planted on her cheek said so, and the way she looked into his eyes made it pretty clear.

We finally moved to the crowded area where the pool was. I had never witnessed so many sexy women in bikinis in one place. Music thumped in the background and huge fire pits and torches lit up that backyard like we were somewhere in Hawaii. I finally got my special fried rice, and it was made by chefs who catered to everyone's individual wants. Jaylin had the Peking duck, and as we took our seats in a lounging area, it wasn't long before others joined us, particularly females. I barely had time to eat. Jaylin and I hadn't said one word to each other, because we were indulged in conversations with women who had plenty of inquiries:

"What's your name?"

"Where do you live?"

"What do you do? Are you married?"

"Why are you here? Weren't you that famous lawyer on TV?"

"Are you interested?"

This was enough to swell any man's head, and the compliments just kept on coming:

"You're very handsome. I love your waves."

"You smell so good."

"You're rocking that suit."

"Your lips are so sexy."

"Take your clothes off. Let's go for a swim."

I was blown away, and it had been a long time since I'd been to one of these parties. I wasn't taking my clothes off to swim, but I did make the women feel comfortable with my conversation. We laughed, drank plenty of alcohol, and chowed down. One chick reached out to feed me teriyaki chicken on a stick.

"Oh my God. Jonathan, you have to taste this," she said, already having the chicken close to my lips. "This is better than the cashew chicken, I promise."

I tasted the teriyaki chicken. She was right. She went to get me more while the others stood around treating me as if I were a king. I couldn't help but to look at Jaylin, who was looking at me, shaking his head. A smirk was on his face, and I certainly knew what that was all about. He got back to conversing with numerous women and men who were near him. The woman from earlier stood directly in front of him, as if she was attempting to keep distance between him and the others. I was surprised that he hadn't moved her out of the way, but as close as her ass was to him, maybe he didn't want her to move. I quickly thought about how Shane had disappeared. I hadn't seen the brother since he was on the stairs.

"Jonathaaaan," the lovely woman sang as she headed my way with more teriyaki chicken on a stick. "Open your mouth, sweetheart. Wide."

I opened my mouth and had never received anything so juicy. I had to thank the woman, so I quickly kissed her on the lips for being so kind. Her eyes bugged. She smiled at me with polished white teeth.

"You're welcome," she said. "I hope to get more of that later."

The way I felt, she absolutely would. I downed several more glasses of alcohol, and the last thing I remembered was being whisked away by the woman who fed me the chicken. After that, I didn't remember shit.

Bright sun beamed through the wide windows in the bedroom, causing me to squint. I was awakened by soft knocks on the door. My body was aching so badly that I could barely get out of the bed to see who it was. A crisp white sheet covered me, and to my left was the woman I had come to the room with. To my right was another woman. I had no idea, whatsoever, who she was.

Trying not to wake them, I eased out of bed then searched around for my clothes. They were here and there. I snatched up my pants, and as I bent over to get them, my head throbbed. I squeezed it to soothe the pain, but the only thing that could help me right now was aspirin. The knock came again, so I hurried to put on my pants then I cracked the door open. Shane was on the other side with a crooked smile on his face.

"Hey, man. Can you wrap it up in about ten or fifteen minutes? We need to check out of here."

"Yeah," I said in a groggy tone. I cleared my throat, as something felt clogged in it. Maybe the chicken. "Give me a minute. I'll be out there soon."

I closed the door then looked at the two women in bed, lying naked. Empty bottles of alcohol were all over the place, pillows were on the floor with sheets, clothes, condoms, even food. I never thought I would be in a situation where I didn't know what in the hell had occurred. This felt real awkward to me, and I was too old for this shit. Not only that, but I had a reputation to protect.

I tiptoed around the room, gathering my things. I couldn't find my cell phone, but I soon spotted it in the corner, next to a trash can. I picked it up then tucked it into my pocket. Afterward, I looked out of the windows, seeing several people chilling by the pool. Jaylin was down there, fully dressed as he sat on a lounging chair with his cell phone up to his ear. Tinted shades covered his eyes, and, to no surprise, the same woman was lying next to him in a thong bikini. I backed away from the window, wondering if anyone had seen the action that had taken place in this room last night. With no walls, and mostly windows, I was sure somebody knew more than me.

I quietly opened the door to leave. When I glanced downstairs, the entire place looked as if a tornado had blown through it. It was a mess. Several people were still downstairs, and I spotted Shane close by the door. He was texting someone. I walked up, and seconds later he put his phone in his pocket.

"You ready?" he said.

"Ye . . . yeah. I think so."

Shane grabbed my shoulder then squeezed it. "Are you all right? You look out of it. Do you need anything?"

"Some aspirin and a bed where I can stretch out. That's what I need."

"I'll take care of that once we get back to Jay's crib. Let me go get him. He's ready to check out of here too."

Shane walked away while I headed outside to get some fresh air. I stood on the wide porch that had stone columns bigger than the ones at the White House. I sucked in a heap of air then cocked my stiff neck from side to side. A row of expensive cars were parked in the curved driveway, so I made my way to Jaylin's truck. As I leaned against it, I saw him and Shane exit the house. The woman who had been hanging on

Jaylin like glue was close behind them. Before coming to the car, he turned to say something to her. Shane unlocked the doors, and we both got inside: me in the front, him in the back.

"So, I heard you had yourself a good time," he said, patting me on the back.

"From what I can remember, yes, I did have a good time. What about you?"

"Always, my brotha. Mr. Chan knows how to throw a party."

"Yes, indeed."

Jaylin kissed the chick on her forehead, watching as she walked away. He then got in the car and straightened his shades. "Well, well, well," he said. "John-John, you definitely went all out last night. Glad you had a good time. You certainly deserved to."

"Like I told Shane, I had a superb time, but after going into that bedroom, I don't remember shit."

Jaylin laughed then drove off. "That's because you had too much to drink. I saw you tossing back the Henny like it was water. I started to stop you, but you looked as if you were having a good time. I didn't want to interfere; after all, you are a grown-ass man who is much older than me."

I laughed at his jab. "Older and much, much wiser. You should have stopped me from tossing it back like that. I mean, the whole thing was wild. No more teriyaki chicken for me in a long time."

"That's what probably got you," Shane said. "And trust me when I say people do spike the chicken."

"Possibly. And all I'm saying is it's odd that I can't remember a thing. I don't even know if I had sex, but I suspect that the two of you did."

"What?" they said in unison.

"Y'all heard me. I observe my surroundings rather well. All I'm gon' say is slick, slick, slick."

"And all I'm gon' say is wrong, wrong, wrong," Shane said.

I turned to look at him. "Man, you did a disappearing act. Didn't nobody see you all night. The last time I saw you, though, things were looking up. You can't sit there and tell me you didn't make a move with the chick you were conversing with on the stairs."

Shane sat back and crossed his arms. "I should plead the Fifth, but the truth is we stepped away to talk about her ailing father. She got emotional and didn't want others to see her cry. I was there for support."

Jaylin snickered underneath his breath. I shook my head while calling Shane out. "Save that sob story for your wife. I'm not sure if she'll buy that bullshit. Even I'm not convinced."

"Well, it's the truth. I keep telling y'all I'm capable of having conversations with beautiful women and not having sex with them. I don't know why that's so hard to believe."

I looked at Jaylin. He shrugged. "Some men can, some men can't," he said. "And some men are some lying muthafuckas who need to quit."

"Exactly," I said.

Shane kept quiet on that subject and started to talk to Jaylin about the deal from yesterday. While that discussion took place, I reached for my phone to see if anyone had called. There were several text messages from my secretary, one message from Crissy, Sylvia had called, and so had Britney. I responded to all of them, saying that I was in Detroit and would call when I got home. After the last text, something alerted me to hit my camera button. I did, and immediately got the shock of my life. Pictures from last night appeared. I quickly swiped through all twenty-eight of them, feeling shameful. So shameful that I deleted the pictures. I didn't say one word to Shane or Jaylin, and when we got back to his house, I was too hyped to go to sleep as planned. I did take some aspirin, but I lay in bed wondering if more pictures would surface.

Less than two days later, I returned to St. Louis. The shit hit the fan. Pictures from that night were blasted on the news, and I suspected they were all over the Internet. I sat stone-like on the edge of my bed, watching the news. One of my socks was in my hand and my jaw dropped as many people weighed in:

"How can you be an upstanding attorney like that and put yourself out there like this?"

"Jonathan Taylor has a sex addiction. He should be arrested for coaxing those young ladies into this."

"Some of you may find these videos offensive. Please beware."

"The attorney who was credited with putting two St. Louis police officers behind bars now finds himself in a sex scandal."

My home phone started ringing off the hook. So did my cell phone. I thought I recognized the number, so I quickly answered it.

"Is this the attorney with the big dick? If so, I need some representation."

The caller laughed then hung up. My phone rang again and again. I didn't answer. I hurried to check the Internet. Many of the pictures were posted on popular social media Web sites. They were blurred, but I was so sure that many were not. I was numb as hell. There was no way in hell I could go to work with all of this going on. More so, I couldn't even go into a courtroom today and try to defend any of my clients. This was a big mess that I didn't see coming. I was mad at myself. Mad at Jaylin for inviting me. and mad at whoever the hell was responsible for leaking those pictures. I called Jaylin to see if he was aware of what was going on. He answered on the first ring.

"I was just getting ready to call you. This is not good, but it's not bad either," he said. "My suggestion: call Olivia Pope, not me."

I didn't see a damn thing funny. "Man, you should have warned me. I had no idea women like that ran in your circle. You can't tell me that you didn't know they would do something like this."

"John-John, calm down. Yes, there are people out there who will do anything for money. Those people run in my circle and yours too. What you need to do right now is turn your negative situation into a positive one. Don't hide from it, face it. Embrace your new celebrity status and use it to your advantage. Meanwhile, behind the scenes, we'll find out who was behind this and sue the shit out of them. You gotta know how to play the game, and not let it play you. You feel me?"

"Hell, yeah, I do and it's something that I tell my clients all the time, but I never thought I'd be on this side of the fence. Just do me a favor and find out who is behind this. I'll go from there."

I ended the call to answer one that I saw from Britney coming in. I couldn't get out one word before she spoke up. "Daddy, is that really you? Please tell me it isn't."

I guessed if I could own up to it to my daughter and explain my situation, I could do so with anyone. That included Sylvia, who was at my door around noon, asking for answers. A gang of reporters were outside of my home, trying to get answers too. I was mad as hell about the chaotic scenery, so I hurried Sylvia inside then slammed the door behind her. She came in, side-eying me as if she had a knife in her purse to cut me.

"Really, Jonathan. Since when did you become a male whore?"

"I'm going to release a statement soon. Until then, I really don't have anything to say."

Sylvia's face twisted. She snapped at me. "To hell with your statement. Don't you feel as if you owe me an explanation now?"

"To be honest with you, I don't. I don't have time to stand here and argue with you either. My reputation is on the line. I don't want my business to suffer because of it. That's what's on my mind right now. That's what's important."

She threw her hands up in the air. "Fine then. Save your business and save yourself. I'm done, Jonathan. I am once and for all done with this."

She swung the door open and ran straight into a reporter who asked if she was one of the women in the pictures and videos. Sylvia didn't answer. She hurried to her car to leave. As another reporter rushed to my door, I shoved him back then slammed the door in his face. I went to my office to write a brief statement that was my defense. Hopefully, it would provide a little damage control. By midday, I released a statement that read:

> *Life brings about many challenges, obstacles, and experiences. During a very difficult time in my life, I resorted to things that I thought would help to put me at ease and cope with a recent, tragic loss in my family. I am deeply saddened that some took advantage of me throughout my darkest days, and I am equally appalled that their actions were done to obtain money.*

Those individuals will face charges, but in the meantime, I apologize to my staff, as well as to my clients, who have always seen me as a respectable, upstanding attorney. I will continue to offer professional legal services to individuals in need, and I thank everyone for their understanding during this unfortunate time.

CHAPTER 24

SYLVIA

I didn't even know Jonathan had gone to Detroit. When I discovered he was with Jaylin, that explained everything. I couldn't believe what my eyes had witnessed on TV, as well as on the Internet. Jonathan had put himself in a bad light. Many people respected him for assisting to put those dirty cops behind bars, and everybody in need was trying to obtain his services. I wasn't sure if that would be the case now.

As far as I could see it, he had fucked up. The comments online were not in his favor, until he released his statement. The tide started to turn, just a little, as people wondered exactly what had happened. The video and pictures were ugly. Nasty, trifling, and ugly. It looked as if some *Fifty Shades* shit was going on, and I had never known Jonathan to play around with toys.

That's why I figured it was probably a setup. But the way he spoke to me this morning, I wasn't having it. Enough was enough. The least he could have said was sorry, and yet again, there I was feeling dissed by him. I felt jealous as hell, and it seemed so out of character for him to put himself in a predicament like that with two women. Lord knows what else happened that day, and he could've made this much easier for me, had he been willing to tell me what the hell had really happened. It hurt that he didn't even think I deserved to know. That spoke volumes about where things really stood between us.

I tried to get some work done, but everybody was gossiping. I was saddened by all of the negative comments, and stupid me wanted to defend his ass. I kept my mouth shut, only because I knew that Jonathan would some way or somehow handle the mess he'd gotten himself into. He was always at his best when under pressure, and he was known as one of the best lawyers in St. Louis because handling crises was his specialty. With that being said, he still had a lot of haters around here. Crissy's mouth was the loudest. She couldn't stop talking about his actions, and the name calling was ridiculous. Deep down, I was mad at her for speaking so ill about him.

"Stupid fuck," she said, standing near my desk. "He's an idiot, and a freaking whore. How are you handling all of this? Did you know he was screwing around with other women?"

I shrugged as if I really didn't care. I certainly didn't want anyone to know, not even Crissy, how damaged behind this I really was. "I mean, what do you want me to say, Crissy? I don't like to see him carrying on like that, but I believe he was taken advantage of, to some extent. I know Jonathan very well. That stuff seems out of character for him, but if you're asking me if I'm mad about it, hell yes, I am. But what can I do about it? I'm not his wife, nor am I considered his girlfriend."

Crissy pursed her lips. "Yeah, and for you not to have *any* status when it comes to him is such a shame. He has you soooo snowed. That statement he released was a bunch of lies. He hasn't experienced a family loss, and when did the dark days come about? Now, I do believe that those chicks saw an opportunity and took it, but Jonathan put himself in that situation, and you can't deny that."

I wanted to slap Crissy across her face for elaborating on the issue with my "status," but I let her slide. Her words stung because there was much truth to them. It was a shame, and I couldn't be completely mad at her for telling it like it was.

"Yes, he did put himself in that situation, but you know what? Who cares? Everybody is around here talking about this like Jonathan is the President of the United States. He's only the president of this company. I doubt that will change."

Crissy winked at me. "It may change. We have to see how this will play out. If our business starts to suffer because of it, you'd better believe he will be asked to step down."

Crissy flung her hair to the side then told me she was leaving. I was glad to hear that. All I wanted was peace right now, but I didn't get it. The phones were ringing off the hook, and somebody from the media had the nerve to call and ask me if I would give an interview to discuss my relationship with the tongue-turning attorney. That's the name she'd given Jonathan, after watching the video.

"Hell, no," I shouted into the phone. "And don't call me again."

I slammed the phone down then started to type again. After completing a letter, I saw a text message flash across my phone. It was from Dana, and it simply said: call me.

I wasn't in the mood to speak to her, but this wasn't the first time she had called. I figured she must have heard or seen what was going on too, so I put aside my bitterness and called her.

"Yes, Dana. What do you want?"

"We need to talk like now. It's urgent. I've been trying to reach you for a while."

"Yeah, well, I've been busy. I don't have time to be getting slapped or to slap people myself."

"It doesn't have to be like that, but you make it that way. All I want to do is clear my name. I'm tired of you and Jonathan accusing me of doing things that I didn't do. Y'all need to know what's really going on."

Dana had my attention. "Where can we meet?"

"How about Forest Park? Near the art museum, after you get off work."

"That's fine."

We ended the call. I got back to work, wondering what Dana had in her possession that would clear her from what we had expected. It was strange that the harassment had stopped. I figured it was because Lesa and Jonathan had parted ways.

I spotted Dana sitting in a parked car at the art museum. She was looking in the rearview mirror while spreading red lipstick across her lips. She always thought she was some kind of beauty queen. I will never forget the negative and ugly things she said about me when Jonathan chose me over her. According to her, I wasn't pretty enough. I was too brown, too fat, and too uneducated. That's how she'd felt about me all along. I don't know why I ever considered her a real friend. To me, she was a green-eyed devil.

I got out of my car then tapped on the widow so Dana could see me. She was so into herself that she didn't even notice I was standing there. She unlocked her doors then told me to get in on the passenger's side.

"Hello," she said as I sat down. "You look nice."

"I didn't come here to get any compliments from you, Dana. What's going on?"

She cocked her head back. "You know what? I don't understand why you're always so snippy with me. You're the one who stole my husband, but you act as if it was the other way around."

"You sound like a broken record. Every time I see you, you say the same thing. For the last time, I didn't steal him. You lost him, and I took him."

"Yeah, and now he's on TV with his dick in other women, and their pussies locked on his mouth. What in the hell do you have to say about that?"

"Not much. He's not my man anymore, so he can do whatever he darn well pleases."

"He may not be your man, but he's still fucking you. You can't deny that, because I have proof that he is."

Dana was starting to irritate me more. I wasn't sure why she asked me to come here. "Can you speed things along? I have other stuff to do."

"I'm sure it's not to go see Jonathan, because he kicked you out this morning, didn't he? I saw that devilish look in your eyes on television, and I could tell the conversation didn't go well."

I opened the car door to leave. "I'm out, Dana. Gripe to Jonathan about your feelings, because—"

She grabbed my arm. "Okay, I'll stop. Close the door and allow me to get to the real reason why I asked you to meet me."

I hesitated but then slammed the door shut. "You got five minutes. After that, I'm leaving."

She rolled her eyes but calmed her voice. "Jonathan is a snake, and all I ever wanted from you was a sincere apology. You've never given me one, and it has left me so bitter and angry about all that happened. Over the years, I've wished nothing but the worst for the both of you, but then I realized that hating the two of you was doing me no good. After all, since my divorce,

I've been blessed with a wonderful husband, I can purchase anything I want, and I am happier in this marriage than I have ever been before."

"That's great, Dana. Real nice, and you've never offered a sincere apology to me either."

"I never felt as if I owed you one, but here's what's up. When you and Jonathan started bugging me about trashing your apartment, scratching cars, leaving notes, and all of that other crap, I talked to my husband about it. He decided to look into it. We found out some interesting things that you may need to know."

"Thanks for wanting to share, but I already found out some interesting things too. Crissy hired a private investigator to follow Lesa. We know that she was involved with several men whom she probably paid to do that stuff for her. He saw her getting an abortion, and after her performance in Vegas, we also know that she is wacko. I thought you were the one behind this, and I apologize for getting it wrong, but considering all that we'd been through, I had to include you as a possible person responsible."

"You were wrong then and you're wrong now. Answer these questions for me: Did you ever speak to or meet this so-called private investigator that Crissy hired? Ever see him? Did she ever show you any work that he had done for her?

Any pictures of Lesa and those numerous lovers? What about when she was at the abortion clinic? Did you see the pictures for yourself?"

I thought back to all that Crissy had presented to me, which was nothing. The only thing she showed me on one occasion was a blurred picture of two people in the back seat of a car. I really couldn't make out the picture, but she said it was Lesa. She said everything, and not once had the private investigator talked to me. This was alarming to me, but why would Crissy lie?

A sheen of sweat started to form on my forehead. I didn't like this feeling I had, and my stomach was starting to hurt.

"I haven't seen much evidence, but I trusted that Crissy wouldn't lie about anything like this. She has been nothing but a good friend. She gave me a place to stay, found a job for me in Atlanta, paid my attorney fees, gave me a job . . . everything. I couldn't ask for more from a friend."

"Friends do betray you, Sylvia. Trust me, I know, especially when it comes to men like Jonathan. Crissy has always been in love with him. She found that job for you in Atlanta so that she could get you out of the way. After you moved, she and Jonathan started a brief relationship that went nowhere. She was bitter . . . angry at him for moving on with Lesa. The only person she figured who could stop Jonathan from marrying Lesa was you. So she moved you back here, set you up in a lavish apartment, gave you a good-paying job, and waited for this thing to play out between you and him. She created just enough chaos to get you and him stirred up. Then she threw in a private investigator who didn't exist, and made you believe that Lesa had betrayed him. The truth is Jonathan betrayed her. Lesa hadn't cheated on him, until you came into the picture. She was devastated, and she did allow a model to perform oral sex on her. I spoke to her about all of this. Even though she does seem a little off, there was no abortion. Crissy lied. She used you to feed Jonathan false information about Lesa."

The whole time Dana spoke, I could barely move. I didn't blink, and couldn't even tell if I was breathing. I was in major shock. So much so that Dana waved her hand in my face to knock me out of my trance.

"I . . . I can't believe any of this. Why . . . How are you so sure? Do you have evidence?"

"I figured you would ask."

Dana opened an envelope that showed clear pictures of Jonathan and Crissy displaying intimacy. They were in a car kissing, and one picture showed his hand down her blouse.

"Those pictures were taken a few years ago. I had Jonathan watched because I didn't know how our divorce was going to turn out. If he was going to use my fling, Lewis, against me, I had to get something on him. I never suspected that my sources would come back with pictures of him and Crissy."

Dana pulled out several more pictures, one of Crissy posing with a pit bull, another with her in disguise while at the movie theater. She was next to my car, and when she walked away, the scratch was visible.

"My guy didn't get everything, but he got enough. He helped me put two and two together, and, at this point, what I told you is what we suspect. If you confront her, I don't know if she will be honest about it. But do me a favor: don't call me. I'm not testifying. I'm not acknowledging anything. As far as I'm concerned, we never had this conversation. I want to get on with my life and be done with all of this. Even though I've made plenty of mistakes, I don't regret where I am today."

I felt like one big fool! I should have known something was up with Crissy. The way she stayed in my business and how she reacted to Jonathan said it all. I was damn near speechless.

You reap what you sow, kept popping up in my head. Karma was there, too, but this came back on me in a major way. I could barely look at Dana after this. I didn't know what to say to her. An apology didn't seem good enough, but I went there anyway.

I squeezed my aching forehead then shifted my head to look at her. "I'm so sorry for what I did. I should have let you and Jonathan work through whatever y'all were going through. It was wrong for me to act on my feelings. In doing so, look at where I am today. Girl, this shit is no picnic, and I honestly don't know what I'm going to do. I could strangle the both of them, but I also have to take responsibility for telling Jonathan that crap about Lesa. If I hadn't said a word, they'd probably be married."

"Maybe so, but between us, it wouldn't have lasted. Lesa got issues. She was talking about cutting his throat and chopping his dick off. I believe Jonathan did the right thing by not marrying her, but he may be upset with you for passing on a lie."

"I don't care about him being mad, and even though you want to be done with this, I may need you to back me up. Can you do that for me?"

"Hell, no. This is your battle. Like I said, if anybody calls me, I don't know shit."

Dana stuck to her words. I thanked her for sharing this information. After she drove off, I sat in my car hoping that she now knew my apology was sincere. It was.

CHAPTER 25

JONATHAN

Things had settled down a little. The statement I released surely helped, and so did the numerous interviews I'd done making myself look like the victim. Many were sympathetic to my situation, and once the names of the women were released and their backgrounds were revealed, it wasn't exactly pretty. Some of the shit put out there wasn't even true, but when you knew people who knew other people, it was easy to get things to work in your favor. I was grateful to Jaylin for his assistance.

Two weeks later, I went into the office and faced my entire team. I apologized again and encouraged everyone to cease the gossiping and get to work. We definitely had plenty of it. The photos and videos did more good than harm, and my caseload was increasing by the day. I barely had time to do anything else, and all personal phone calls were ignored. I laughed at the one from Lesa where she took cheap shots at me and claimed how happy she was we didn't get married. Britney's mother, Beverly, had something to say too. She was highly disappointed, and she claimed Britney was ashamed to call me her father. That wasn't the case because I had already spoken to Britney. We were good. Then there was Sylvia again. I figured she wanted to argue and fuss, so I deleted her message. I just didn't have time for it. I doubted that I ever would.

I was sitting behind my desk, taking a ten-minute break. A salad was in front of me, and a cold lemonade drink was to my right. My secretary screened every single call for me, and she buzzed in to tell me that Sylvia was there to speak to me. I thought about telling her I was busy, but since I was in the middle of a break, what the hell? She came into my office, looking as if something was deeply troubling her. Her hair was swept back into a ponytail, she wasn't wearing any makeup, and her attire was casual. I didn't think she'd come to work like this, but maybe she was off today.

"I know you're busy," she said, closing the door, "but I had to see you. I promise not to take up much of your time."

"No problem. Have a seat."

Slightly fidgeting, she sat in a chair in front of my desk. Her eyes filled with tears, but she hurried to blink them away.

"I've been so caught up with you that I have completely lost myself," she said. "I'm not going to ramble on about how I managed to get here, but there is something that you need to know. I don't know if it will make a difference to you, but Lesa didn't do all of those things that the so-called private investigator claimed she did. It was all a lie, so the two of you wouldn't get married."

My face was already scrunched. I honestly didn't want to hear much more. "Are you telling me you made that shit up? Is that what you're saying?"

"No. I didn't make it up. Crissy did. She never hired a private investigator like she said she did. She was also the one behind those letters, and she did all of this crazy stuff because of her obsession with you. I never knew the two of you were involved with each other, but now that I know, it all makes sense. Her attitude toward you makes sense. She used me as a pawn to cause harm to your relationship. I had already been doing so by having sex with you while knowing that you were engaged to someone else, so I was an easy target for her. So as of the other day, I quit. She doesn't know it yet, but she will know when she returns today. I don't know how you intend to handle her, and, quite frankly, I don't care. I'm tired of saving you. Now it's time for me to save myself."

I held my breath when she mentioned Crissy. It never dawned on me that she would do something like this, but, as Sylvia had said, it made sense. I remembered asking Crissy to send me the documentation from the private investigator. She never did, and I never followed up with her because I'd been too busy. I didn't even know that she supposedly loved me. We'd only had sex around four or five times. It wasn't that serious.

"I will deal with Crissy today, and I regret that I didn't tell you about my relationship with her. It was very brief, and it didn't occur when I was with—"

Sylvia held up her hand. "Save it, Jonathan. It doesn't matter anymore, but I will say that you are one big hypocrite. All this time you made me feel so guilty about being with Jaylin. He's your friend, but you had no issues with going behind my back and having sex with my so-called friend. All of this has been too much for me. All I can say is I wish you all the best."

She stood then turned to walk to the door. I felt horrible for stringing her along, for not being completely honest about my feelings, and for putting her through this mess. She had a point about my friendship with Jaylin and her friendship with Crissy, but I didn't bother to elaborate on it. I knew that if I told her how I felt right now, like she also said, it wouldn't matter. There was a time when I would be able to relay everything to her and she would understand. Right now, she was hurt. She felt let down. Used. And I couldn't do anything about it but watch her walk out of my office, and, possibly, out of my life for good.

Minutes later, I got up from my desk and marched to the other side of the building to Crissy's office. I wasn't sure if she was there yet, but just as I was coming down the hall, so was she. Sylvia stood waiting for her. From a distance, I saw Crissy walk up to her with a wide smile on her face. That smile vanished when Sylvia slapped the shit out of her. The slap was so hard that she spun around and hit the floor. Sylvia dropped a piece of paper in her lap then walked off. I strutted slowly up to Crissy, who was looking in awe while holding the side of her face.

"Did that bitch just slap me?" she said. "Who in the hell does she think she is?"

I helped Crissy off the floor. To spare us the embarrassment, I asked her to go into her office so we could talk. Several people whispered and watched as we entered her office, closing the door behind us.

"That bitch is fired!" Crissy yelled while still holding her red, swollen face. "Why in the hell did she do that?"

"You can't fire her because she quit. I already think you know why. If you don't, you may want to read that letter in your hand."

She unfolded the letter and began to read it. I hadn't a clue what it said, but whatever was in it caused her eyes to get real big. She swallowed hard then she ripped the letter to shreds, throwing it at me.

"You know why I did this," she said through gritted teeth. Tears ran down her face, as she tried to explain her reasoning. "You know why, Jonathan, and why would you fuck me then ignore me? I wanted you! I needed you after my father died. You made me feel as if I was sooooo freaking special to you. You put the charm on thick, and the next thing I knew, you were off with another bitch, about to marry her. You left me hanging. I didn't know what to doooo!"

I wasn't sure how I felt about this. Crissy was a spoiled brat who got upset when she didn't get her way. She acted that way in business, as well as in her personal life. I couldn't believe that she thought I was serious about being with her, even though she implied her feelings were that deep. For me, it was all about sex. I needed sex after my relationship with Sylvia had failed and she moved to Atlanta. Crissy was my fallback person. She was nothing more, nothing less. I thought I made that clear at the time. Maybe not.

"It's apparent that you're unstable, and I don't want to say the wrong thing. I am, however, sorry if you felt as if I led you on and made you feel as if we had something unique going on. I didn't feel that way."

"Sorry, Jonathan?" She wiped snot from her nose then blew it with a tissue. "Sorry my ass. Keep your fucking sorry. The arrival is too late."

I shrugged. "Maybe so, but it's been said. What has not been said is I want you out of here. Today. Your lies and games have hurt a lot of people, and you could be arrested for doing what you did. I'm not going to press charges, and I'm not going to say a word about this to anyone. That's only if you resign and leave by your own free will."

Crissy plopped back in her chair. She lowered her head into her hands, refusing to look up at me. "Get out, Jonathan. Get the hell out, now!"

"I will, after you tell me your next move. Do I have to call the police, or will you be e-mailing me your resignation letter?"

Crissy sat silent for a minute. She knew that she had no other choice but to resign. I hated that it had to be this way. I wondered, if Mr. Duncan were alive, how he would feel about all of this. Surely, he'd be upset with me for involving myself with his daughter. He'd also be upset with her for carrying on the way she did.

"You'll have your stupid freaking letter," she snapped. "Now, get out!"

I left her office and returned to mine. Her resignation letter arrived almost twenty minutes later. I had security keep an eye on her as she gathered her things to go. Almost two hours later, they informed me that she had left the premises.

While Brian was at work, I loaded Lady and Brady into the car so we could go for a long ride. After all that had happened, from the Hell House chaos to now, I had time to think about how I wanted to make my world a better place. I was still bitter about some things, and I knew that I had to get certain things off my chest in order to move on. Nonetheless, many people in and around St. Louis wanted to know who was in the process of building one of the most extravagant houses our city had ever seen. It was discussed in our office, Brian had asked me about it, and the media mentioned something about it a few weeks back when they gave a tour of the Fedelis house that had been up for sale. It was a $30 million mansion that was up for sale because the owners had been put in jail. Nobody knew who was building a house comparable to that one, but after recalling a conversation with Jonathan a while back, I knew who it was. I needed to clear up some things with Jaylin, so I drove to his new place, hoping that he would be there. Sure enough, when I parked my car I saw him standing outside with several construction workers in orange caps. Jaylin had on one too. He squinted to see who I was. The wind was a little gusty, and some of the dirt and debris was blowing around.

"What the hell?" he said, removing his hat and tucking it underneath his arm. "Why ain't my security system working? Somebody better tell me what is wrong with the security system around here."

One of the men responded, "They're not on while we're here, and the gates stay open so the trucks can get through. Would you like for us to keep them closed?"

"Hell, yeah," he griped as he looked at me coming his way with two dogs on leashes.

I ignored his foolishness and rolled my eyes. Even put on a smile, so he knew I wasn't there to cause trouble. "Hiiii, Jaylin. I came all this way to see you, and this is how you treat me?"

He cut his eyes then walked up to me. "What's the occasion?"

"No special occasion. I just wanted to apologize to you for the way I've been acting toward you. I had you at the top of my hate list, and now I'm removing your name. I've thought about a lot of things that you've said to me, and even though they were pretty harsh, I needed to hear them. I'm so thankful that we got a chance to hook up. I wouldn't trade my little experience for anything."

There was a smirk on his face. "What in the hell have you been smoking? I know you didn't come all the way over here to tell me that. You could have called me on the phone to say that."

"Well, I wanted to see this house everybody's been talking about, too. Care to give me a tour?"

He looked at the dogs as they sniffed the ground. "Do I have to give the dogs a tour too? If they ain't trained, they can stay out here."

I picked up one, then the other. I gave one to Jaylin. "They're trained. And they like to be held, too."

He held the dog while he spent the next several minutes walking me around his new home. Like Jonathan said, it was amazing. We sat near the pool, talking some more and watching the dogs play.

"Cute, well-mannered dogs," he said. "I'm glad my daughter ain't here. She'd have me buying them from you."

"You may be able to buy her anything she wants, but those dogs aren't for sale."

"That's your take on it. I have mine. Now, why haven't you spoken to Jonathan?"

"I guess you have, huh?"

"Yes, I have. He told me about everything that happened. Sorry it turned out that way."

"I'm not sorry. It needed to happen, just like the sex between us needed to happen, too."

Jaylin stroked the hair on his chin, as if he were in thought. "Uh, I'm not so sure about that, but then again, you did need it way more than I did."

I couldn't help but to laugh at this fool. He was so full of it, but at the time, I guess I did. "I did need it. I needed to upset Jonathan, hook back up with him, encourage him to break up with his fiancée, meet back up with Dana . . ."

"I get it. It was all in the plan. We don't always know why things happen, but one day we discover why."

"Absolutely, my friend."

Jaylin moved his head from side to side. "No more friends. I already got too many, but you can always go on the waiting list."

I playfully shoved his shoulder. "No, thanks. I'm good."

We conversed for a little while longer then he walked me to my car. As I put the dogs in the back seat, Jaylin held the door open.

"Call Jonathan," he said. "Don't completely depart from the man, and the least you two can be is close friends."

"I agree, but not now, Jaylin. We can't be close friends, but one day we may be able to and mean it."

He nodded then opened his arms to give me a tight hug. It felt good to put closure to one more thing that had been bothering me. Now it was time for me to carry on with my life. I drove away with a smile on my face, feeling good about where things were headed. This time, I was going to get it right!

CHAPTER 27

JONATHAN

Crissy was out. Sylvia was gone. Lesa was no more, and Dana was remarried. I was perfectly fine with all of the above. I had some soul searching to do, especially after this thing with Crissy went so far left that I didn't even see it coming. The truth was I had hurt a lot of people. I had been hurt too, but it was always wise to get to the root of the problem and figure out why the same shit kept repeating itself. That's what I did. I'd always had an urge to be married. That's what my parents represented to me, so I wanted what they had. But what they had took patience, commitment, compromise, love, respect, and honesty. I wasn't all the way there yet.

One big problem with me was that a woman would always be second to my career. Many wouldn't accept that. Dana didn't, so she found herself in the arms of another man. Lesa wouldn't have accepted it either, and Sylvia surely had her complaints about it, but I loved my job. It took priority over everything. I spent years and years building my empire. Maybe I was being a little selfish, but for now that's how it had to be.

I was in the kitchen eating a sandwich and reading notes from a case that was due to start next week. The doorbell rang, and I was slightly perturbed about being interrupted. I made my way to the door with a frown on my face. Through the wavy, blurred glass, I could see a couple of people standing on the porch, but I didn't know who they were. I assumed they were some people from the media, but when I pulled the door open, there stood Britney, along with a young man holding a baby. Britney and he smiled at me, but my expression remained flat. I was a little confused. I was definitely happy to see my daughter, so I invited them in and quickly embraced her. She was still beautiful as ever. Her natural hair had grown longer. It was thick and fluffy as it hung past her shoulders. She had picked up a little weight, too, and as I thought about her appearance, I pulled away from her then looked at the baby.

"We named him after you," she said to me. "Well, his first name anyway. His middle name is Dayon, and his last name is Wilford. That's my last name too. I want to introduce you to my husband and one-month-old son."

"Hello, Mr. Taylor," the young man said.

I staggered backward, damn near falling. I almost thought I didn't hear her correctly, but I knew I had. Of course I was happy, but I had so many questions swarming in my head that I couldn't even respond to her. Britney reached for my hand, clenching it together with hers. She pulled me over to the couch, where I took a seat. She sat next to me, while the young man sat in another chair with the baby.

"I know this is very shocking to you, but please don't be mad at me, Daddy. I haven't been home to see you because I got pregnant. I wanted to keep going to law school, but with all that was going on, I had to quit. I don't know if I'm going to return, because that little boy needs me as a full-time mother right now. I love him to death, as I do my husband. I wanted so badly to tell you this, but I figured you wouldn't understand. You had high hopes for me, but my being a lawyer was always your dream, not mine. Please, please, don't be upset with me, and if it's okay with you, I want to move back home. Dayon was just offered a job here. We want to move back here with our baby. We may have to stay with you for a while, but I promise you that we'll do everything to get on our feet and move out as soon as we can."

Britney said a mouthful. I massaged my forehead and tapped my foot on the floor. Looked at Dayon then at my grandson. Turned to my daughter and could only ask her why.

"Why didn't you just tell me what was going on? All you had to do was call me, Britney. I don't like to be kept in the dark like this, and why couldn't you just complete school?"

She shrugged. "Sometimes we don't know why, Daddy, but things happen and you just gotta go with the flow. You're not always the easiest person to talk to. As busy as you be, sometimes I feel as if you have to put me on your schedule. I've always said that to you, but it is what it is. School will always be there, but for now, my child is what's important."

As much as I may have wanted to scream at her for not going to college and doing what I anticipated that she would do, there was nothing that I could say or do to change this situation. Britney had her mind made up; it was obvious. Even so, the marriage thing was a bit much for me to swallow. Why get married at such a young age, when neither one of them had direction?

I looked at Dayon to address him. "Don't sit there all quiet and let my daughter speak for you.

Tell me what the plan is. What are you prepared to do about this situation, and what kind of sacrifices are you prepared to make?"

Appearing slightly nervous, he sat up straight then cleared his throat. "I was in law school too, but it has been rough with the baby and everything. He and Britney are my priority. I truly believe that I need to step up, get a job, and take care of my family. I was offered a job at an investment firm last week. The pay is good, but we need to save some money. We don't have any money saved, and it's been a struggle. I told my parents about my decision, but they aren't supportive of it. They need time, and I get that. Like you, they had high hopes for me, but what they don't understand is that this is my life. It swung this way and now I have to roll with it."

Even if I didn't want to, so did I. There was no way in hell that I would ever disown my daughter. I would never turn her or my grandson away, and the way I looked at it, the timing of this couldn't have been more right. Whenever I was down, there was always something pertaining to Britney that would swoop into my life and lift me up. She just didn't know how special she was to me. I was the luckiest father in the world.

I spent the next few hours getting to know more about the young man my daughter had married, all while holding my grandson in my arms. It was such a good feeling. As he squirmed around in my arms, my thoughts were all over the place. I wondered if there was anything else I could have done as a father. I thought about the many times my daughter said she'd felt neglected. I even thought about the pressure I put on her to do what I wanted her to do. I wasn't going to be hard on her or myself, because the truth of the matter was that some things were destined.

Later that night, Britney put the baby to sleep and came into my room with a checkerboard set. She sat on my bed and we started to play, just like we used to when she was little.

"I've gotten good at this," she said, rubbing her hands together. "And if you think you're going to beat me, you may want to think again."

"You may be good, but never as good as me."

I allowed her to make the first move; I made the next. After several more moves, I found myself in the hole, contemplating how to get out of it.

"The only person who can beat me at this game is Sylvia," she said. "I can't wait for her to see my baby. When can I invite her over?"

"As you know, we are not speaking to each other right now. She's doing her thing; I'm doing mine. I don't think it would be a good idea for her to come over here."

Britney pursed her lips and crossed her arms. "She can still be doing her thing and come over here, can't she?"

"I guess, but let's wait a while. I have my reasons for waiting, so please don't go behind my back and do anything crazy. Respect my decision."

"I will, but you need to hurry up and work through this stuff so the two of you can get married. I will be glad when y'all grow up and do the right thing."

I had to laugh. Britney had always been determined to see me and Sylvia together. She was convinced that we would one day be husband and wife. I wasn't.

"That day will never come," I said. "Sorry to shatter your dreams and break your heart."

"You're the one who taught me to never say never. And after what I presented to you today, how can you say that? I bet you *never* thought I would show up at your doorstep with a husband and baby, did you? And you *never* thought that I would be five seconds away from winning this game, did you?"

Britney cleaned house. I lost the game that fast, only because I wasn't focusing.

"Well, if you put it like that then I guess anything is possible. I will never say never again."

She high-fived me and demanded that we play another game.

"That's what I'm talking about," she said. "Anything, my dear Daddy, is possible."

She was so right, but I still felt comfortable saying to myself that I was happy with how things had turned out, and I had a feeling that Sylvia was too.